THE PRIME MINISTERS

To Nellie

— Ronald 84

THE PRIME MINISTERS

WILLIAM RONALD

EXILE EDITIONS

TORONTO

All photographs of William Ronald
are by JOHN REEVES. All photographs of the paintings
are by JIM CHAMBERS.

This edition is published by Exile Editions Limited, 69 Sullivan
Street, Toronto, Canada, in association with the Art Gallery of
Ontario. The publisher wishes to acknowledge the Canada
Council and the Ontario Arts Council for financial assistance
towards publication

ISBN 0-920428-52-5

For
Helen,
Suzanne and Dianna,
Bradley and Shannon,
the prime ministers
of my heart.

I am indebted to Colin MacLeod
and Professor John Saywell for their advice
and hard work on all matters
of history. The paintings
are not reproduced in exact historical
order so that the triptychs could
be presented in just proportion.
The sizes of the paintings
are given in feet and inches: metric
may now be the mode,
but I see things in feet and inches.

A special note of appreciation to
Aiko Suzuki and Ron Atkey and Senator Peter Stollery
and John Morris.

And thanks to my old friend,
Barry Callaghan, who always helps
me make it through the night.

THE PRIME MINISTERS

Sir John A. Macdonald	1867–1873, 1878–1891
Alexander Mackenzie	1873–1878
Sir John Abbott	1891–1892
Sir John Thompson	1892–1894
Sir Mackenzie Bowell	1894–1896
Sir Charles Tupper	1896
Sir Wilfrid Laurier	1896–1911
Sir Robert Borden	1911–1920
Arthur Meighen	1920–1921, 1926
William Lyon Mackenzie King	1921–1926, 1926–1930, 1935–1948
Richard B. Bennett	1930–1935
Louis St. Laurent	1948–1957
John G. Diefenbaker	1957–1963
Lester B. Pearson	1963–1968
Joseph Clark	1979–1980
Pierre Elliott Trudeau	1968–1979, 1980–

PREFACE

I AM A PAINTER. I was born in a small Ontario town. I've always had a certain advantage. I've looked at the large world with a small town wonder, the large world of men on stage, taking hold of their own destinies by the scruff of the neck. I love men and women who take hold of their destinies. So, a few years ago, I decided to paint the portraits of sixteen such men, the Prime Ministers, the men who had ministered to this country. The idea filled me with a sense of wonder. Who were they? What had they done? How had they shaped me, and how would I shape them? I began to read and read. I wanted to read through their worlds and come out the other end, to the nub of their character and how I saw them. I am not a historian, but along the way I put together little histories so I'd have a sense of their place in time, the face of how things had happened to them. And then, as each began to inhabit me, I painted their portraits. They live in me. I live in them. The portraits and those little histories are here, and also short reflections on each portrait, what I think I see when I see how I saw them.

THE PRIME MINISTERS

$6\frac{1}{2}' \times 15'$

SIR JOHN A. MACDONALD

$6\frac{1}{2}' \times 5'$ ALEXANDER MACKENZIE

3′ × 3′   SIR JOHN ABBOTT

4′ × 3′

SIR JOHN THOMPSON

28″ × 28″   SIR MACKENZIE BOWELL

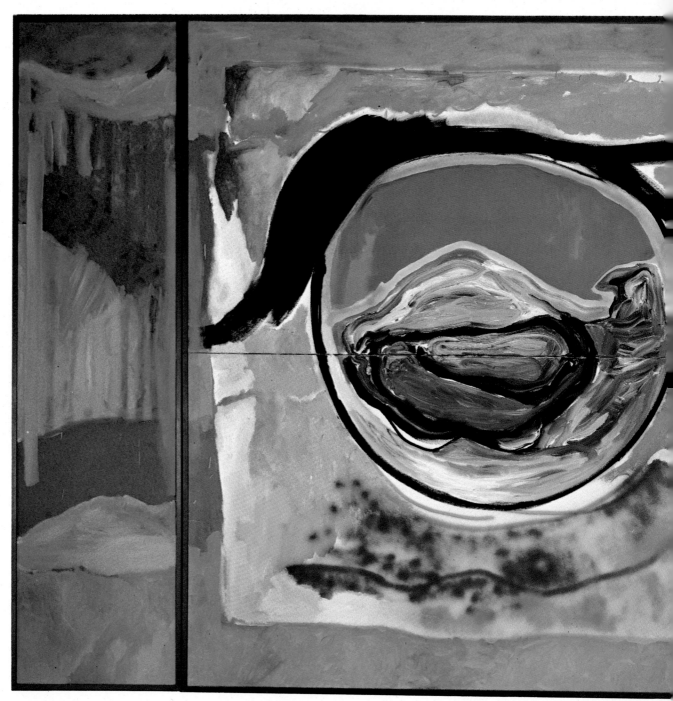

8′ × 12′

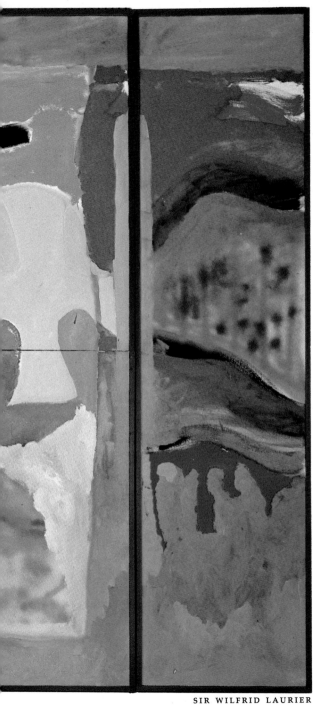

SIR WILFRID LAURIER

4' × 3'

SIR CHARLES TUPPER

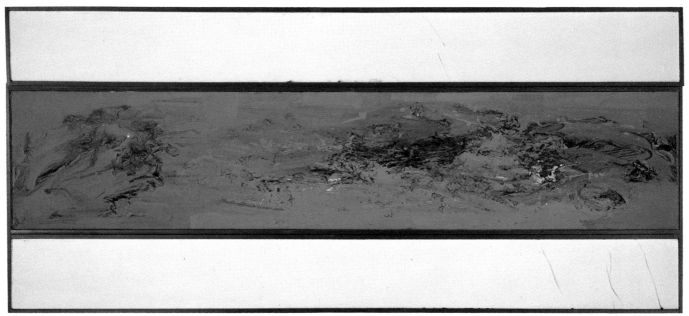

4′ × 12′

SIR ROBERT BORDEN

5' × 11'3"

WILLIAM LYON MACKENZIE KING

7′ × 3½′

ARTHUR MEIGHEN

$6\frac{1}{2}' \times 5'$

RICHARD B. BENNETT

$6\frac{1}{2}' \times 5'$

LOUIS ST. LAURENT

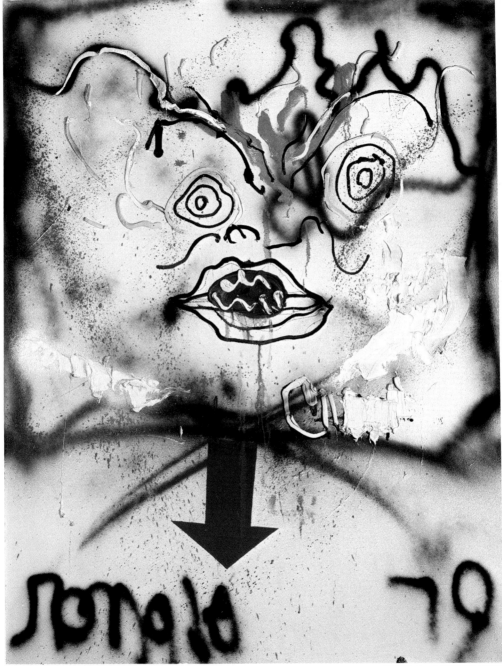

6½′ × 5′   JOHN G. DIEFENBAKER

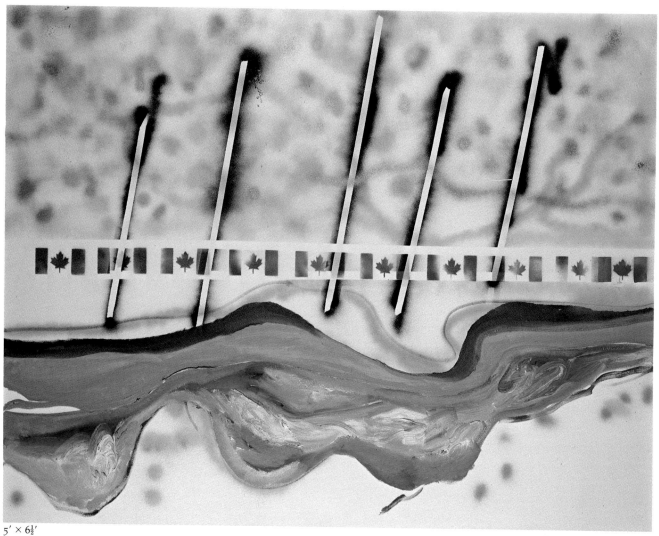

5' × 6½'

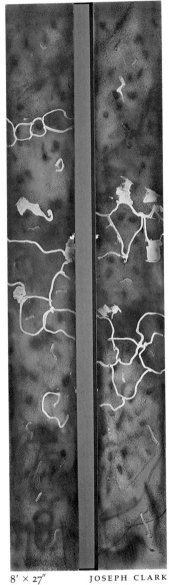

8′ × 27″   JOSEPH CLARK

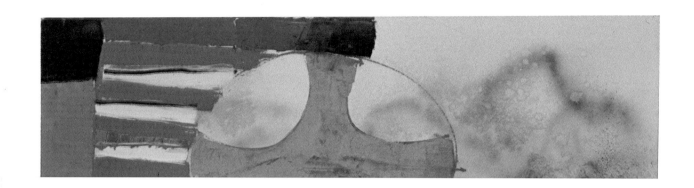

ONLY MACDONALD can be called Father of the Nation. He strides across Canadian history. He brought the nation into existence, gave it a structure and developed strategies that enabled it to survive. Like all successful Prime Ministers, he was a consummate politician. History has made him a statesman, but he would have rejected that pretentious title as the bunk. To him, politics was getting and keeping power, an art he practised with skill equalled by few others. He had principles and set objectives, but he felt men who stuck to their principles often sank with them, and men who moved too quickly toward objectives all too often ended up in opposition. Twist and turn, a double shuffle, give and take – these were the tools of his trade. Procrastinate, procrastinate, so he was called Old Tomorrow. His devices weren't elegant, but they were effective. So, too, was a Senate appointment or a snort of whiskey when it came time to buy votes.

Macdonald took the world as it came, imperfect, and he was prepared to make use of imperfections when it suited him. You forgave men their shortcomings – unless it was disloyalty to the party – and you accepted slings and slurs with good grace. As he wrote to one anxious colleague: "Take things pleasantly and when fortune empties her chamber pot on your head, smile and say 'We are going to have a summer shower.'" His vocabulary could be as colorful as his youth – when he went to the U.S. with a friend, the friend dressed as a bear while he played the concertina and collected money in a hat, money for whiskey. His drinking was notorious. In the House of Commons, where drunken scenes were not uncommon and there was often good reason for the wide aisle separating government and opposition, Macdonald's water glass was sometimes filled with gin, sometimes with whiskey. On one occasion he was sick on the public platform, and on another, engaged in a drunken brawl with his opponent during a political meeting. There were also times when he disappeared. Once, he missed the arrival of the Governor General in Halifax because he was in his room drinking port and reading dime novels. When wakened, he cried, "Vamoose from this ranch," something he did himself in 1886 when he rode down the Fraser Canyon on the C.P.R. locomotive's cow-catcher. His wife was with him on the cow-catcher and he was seventy-one and still full of beans.

Macdonald had reason to drink. He married at 28, but his first wife was an invalid and, as she needed the southern sun, they were often separated. His first son died in infancy, although a second survived but never seemed close to his father. After his wife's death, he remained a bachelor for a decade and then married a woman little more than half his age. Their daughter was born crippled and retarded, so there was a melancholy about the house, and a sadness as the old man, a little tipsy, regularly came home late from the Commons and read aloud to a daughter who never became a woman.

Macdonald's life centered on the Conservative Party and the House of Commons. To him, the party was a living, breathing organism that needed constant care. It had to reflect the diversity of the divided country: Catholics and Orangemen, wets and drys, Québec nationalists and Ontario imperialists, farmers and manufacturers. It was not easy, demanding continual compromise and the incessant use of personal and constituency – even provincial – patronage to keep the troops in line. Gratitude – less politely, patronage and even bribery – were part of the political system, and to Macdonald's generation it was naive or hypocritical to assume it could be otherwise. He denounced the secret ballot, introduced by the Holier-Than-Thou Liberals, because it encouraged deceit: how could you tell if the bribed voter had kept his promise? Open voting was manly; secret voting threatened the system.

Macdonald was at ease in the Commons, where he sat for almost fifty years. He was not a great orator or debater, but he had an easy style, an engaging manner, a way of diluting attack with an irrelevant (often irreverent) or hopelessly exaggerated response that enraged the opposition. There were times when you had to attack the opposition, you could never persuade them. There were times when they tested endurance: "I can lick you quicker than hell can scorch a feather," he once shouted across the House. But far more important, he kept his supporters happy and loyal: "McQuade, you spoke like an angel," he told a backbencher whose dreary speech had emptied the House. "I am proud of you."

Macdonald was born in Scotland, and came to Canada as a five-year-old to settle with his family in Kingston. He became a lawyer without a university education – for there was none – and in 1844, was elected to the legislature. The colony was a union of Ontario and Québec (or Canada West and Canada East), equally represented, and politics was the art of balancing the needs and greed of each, finding combinations of French and English, Grits and Tories, to form and maintain government.

By the late 1850s and early 1860s, the British colonies in North America faced an uncertain future. Political deadlock paralyzed government. The American civil war brought enormous prosperity, but it also brought danger. Britain seemed sympathetic to the south, and wise men feared that after the war the victorious north would turn its battle-tested veterans against the defenceless colonies – Manifest Destiny with one brutal stroke. And there was a haunting economic question: losing their preferred position in the British market after Britain adopted free trade, the colonies had locked into a reciprocity treaty with the United States – for the products of farms, forests, and fisheries. But would an angry Washington renew that treaty after the war? Chances seemed slim.

In Canada, the alternatives were clear: simply dissolve the union, or in dissolving it, try to find a solution to all the problems facing the colonies – above all ensuring the political survival of British North America. Macdonald's choice was emphatic: create a general confederation of all the British colonies, create a new rival state in North America, stretching from sea to sea.

At Charlottetown in 1864, the Canadians urged the Maritime colonies, gathered to discuss their future, to consider a broader union. Weeks later at Québec, the grand design of a Canadian federation was worked out. Macdonald was unable to convince either his Québec colleagues or the Maritimers that only a single strong government could keep control of the northern half of the continent. He was, however, able to sketch out the constitution for such a country in which the central government would legislate for peace, order and good government. But, resistance to the proposed federation was strong – everywhere except Ontario. Cartier, his Québec lieutenant, was able to swing the majority behind Confederation, but at first New Brunswick balked, Nova Scotia later elected only one supporter, and Prince Edward Island refused to join. But with Macdonald's leadership, British pressure, and, on occasion, the temptations of Canadian gold, opposition was circumvented or overcome. The Dominion of Canada was born on July 1, 1867. Macdonald, dubbed Sir John A. for the occasion, was the obvious and only choice as Prime Minister of the new nation.

His first great task was to complete the framework, and move west before American trade, squatters, and ranchers dominated the largely unsettled lands between the Great Lakes and the Rockies, owned by the Hudson's Bay Company for over two hundred years. With British help, Macdonald bought the west for a song in 1869 (compared to what the Americans paid Russia for Alaska, the quick "Yankee" traders were really in Ottawa). But the inhabitants of Red River – on which Winnipeg now rests – were not so ready to be bought and sold. Led by Louis Riel, the métis – offspring of French and a few English fur-traders and Indian mothers – took up arms and formed a provisional government, demanding that Macdonald's government guarantee the protection of the French language and Catholic schools in a province where, for the moment at least, the métis were in control. In the end, Riel had his way. The negotiations were punctuated by Riel's execution of Thomas Scott, a Canadian bigot and trouble-maker. Once concluded, Macdonald sent an army to Manitoba – just in case. And – just in case – Riel fled as the army approached. It was a wise move. Macdonald and Riel would tangle again.

Macdonald knew there were few links between British Columbia and Canada, for even his mail came via San Francisco. There were Canadians out there who shared his vision, but there were also many Americans who urged President Grant to follow the 1867 purchase of Alaska by either occupying or buying British Columbia, completing American ownership of the entire Pacific coast. But once

4

again, the British pressed the colonial legislature to deal with the Canadians – and the promise of a healthy financial settlement and a railway to the coast within ten years brought British Columbia into the union in 1871.

Macdonald's problem was to get the railway built, and built before more American settlers moved north. He discovered it was difficult to find Canadians willing and able to undertake such an enormous venture without American backing – and Americans who were interested wanted to scuttle the all-Canadian route. The group that finally got the contract – secretly retaining their American connections – was so grateful that they donated $300,000 to Macdonald's 1872 election fund. As Bessie Smith used to sing about so much wanting and so much taking of money: "You got a hand full of gimmee and a mouth full of much obliged." It was seedy, risky work: old politics as practised by Old Tomorrow. The Pacific Scandal began to break, and when it did, Macdonald was forced to resign, spending the years from 1873 to 1878 in opposition. In a way, he was lucky. The Liberal Prime Minister, Alexander Mackenzie, was left to wrestle with the intractable problems of a world-wide depression.

In opposition, Sir John A. and his colleagues, notably the Nova Scotia War Horse, Charles Tupper, put together the ingredients of the National Policy. Central to the design was a high protective tariff that would protect the Canadian market for Canadian manufacturers, encourage Canadian infant industries, and, paradoxically, attract foreign investors and foreign branch plants. Rapid construction of the Canadian Pacific Railway would ensure the flow of goods east and west across the country. And an active immigration policy, Macdonald promised, would fill the grainlands of the west, providing wheat for export and markets for Canadian industry. The rhetoric of the National Policy promised some solution to the depression. Mackenzie had none and Macdonald returned to office in 1878, remaining there for thirteen years.

Designed largely by businessmen, the tariff walls went up in 1879, and many are still there. A group of Scots Canadians (like Macdonald) – backed by the Bank of Montreal – formed the C.P.R., hired American engineers, imported labour from the United States,

Europe, and China, raised money in Britain and the States, and built the CPR not in ten years but in five – rewarded for their efforts by millions in cash and millions of acres in the prairies and British Columbia. It was one of the great engineering feats of the nineteenth century. And immigrants did move west – first to Manitoba and then a trickle behind the lines of steel into the territories. But the world was not ready for the Canadian west: there were still farm lands on the more accessible American frontier; there was little demand in a depression-ridden world for Canadian wheat; and Canadian scientists had yet to find the wheat that could survive the inhospitable prairie climate.

But western settlement was still large enough to threaten the life of the métis, many of whom had moved west to the banks of the South Saskatchewan. They and their Indian relatives found the new life on the reservations, schooled in the ways of western agriculture, strange and intolerable. Even the new white settlers were roused to fury by the benign neglect of Macdonald's government and they, too, encouraged the métis to trek south to Montana, where Louis Riel was teaching school, to persuade him to come north and work a second miracle.

By 1884, Riel did believe in miracles. He had become a prophet, a man destined to create a new church in the west, a man who dealt not with the earthly representatives of the Deity but with God himself. Back in Batoche on the banks of the South Saskatchewan, he assumed the leadership of the dissidents and demanded that Ottawa respond to their many requests. Months passed, and as Macdonald promised only promises, tension mounted, and pressed by his followers, Riel decided that once again military blackmail would work. In the spring of 1885, the métis and their Indian allies took up arms and tomahawk. The rebellion was short and bloody, and within weeks Riel was master of the South Saskatchewan and the alarm bells had rung as far away as Calgary and Edmonton.

They had also rung in Ottawa, where Macdonald was in no mood to yield to blackmail or rebellion. Within days, 8000 men were on their way to the seat of the rebellion over the still unfinished line of the CPR (proving, of course, to militant Ontario that all the expense of the railroad was necessary). It was not a glorious campaign. The Indians could not be organized, the métis were too few in number and too short of supplies, and within a few months, the Canadian troops held Louis Riel, Poundmaker and Big Bear, captive. The rebellion was over; Macdonald's problems had just begun.

The leaders were tried for treason, but it was only against Riel that Macdonald's government firmly pressed its case, sending the best eastern lawyers to the packed Regina courtroom. Riel was found guilty, despite a plea of insanity which he angrily rejected, and despite the jury's recommendation of mercy, he was sentenced to hang. The scene shifted to Macdonald in Ottawa. French Canada identified with Riel, a symbol of the fight for cultural survival; English Canada, recalling the death of Scott and the bloodshed on the frontier, demanded his head. Macdonald was determined that the law should follow its course, a decision reinforced by the cruder political calculation of losses in Ontario or Québec. But he did yield to demands for a medical commission to determine whether Riel was insane. However, when one doctor reported that he was, Macdonald deleted the offending section in the report. Riel was hanged in Regina on November 16, 1885.

Riel's execution was an enormous link in the chain leading to the Parti Québécois, for it not only heightened tensions between French and English but revealed the fundamental differences between their conceptions of the Canadian state. To Macdonald and English Canada, the death of Riel meant that law had triumphed over treason, order over violence, the new Canada over the old. To French Canada, it meant that the English had sought vengeance in hanging only Riel, that the French language and culture were safe only in Québec, and that a minority is powerless when confronted by a united and determined majority. Their assumptions about the politics of compromise in a bicultural state were rudely shattered.

Any doubts were soon removed when, in 1890, Manitoba, now in the hands of an Anglo-Saxon majority, abolished French language rights and Catholic schools. With religious bigotry and racial animosities on the loose, the national debate focussed not on ways to maintain cultural pluralism, but on how to end it. The basic question, Dalton McCarthy, protestant champion and sometime Imperial federationist, told Macdonald, was "Whether this country is to be English or French." To the Liberal, John Charlton, the answer was clear: "The sentiment that received the greatest applause was when I asserted that a successful French nationality in the North American continent was a hopeless dream, for that question had been settled on the Plains of Abraham."

Macdonald did not live to see the full fury of the debate, for it still rages. But he did see his country tragically divided, and saw his power slip away in Québec in the aftermath of the Riel execution. Québec has been overwhelmingly Liberal ever since.

But he did live long enough to see the first concerted attack on the supremacy of the central government, an attack led by Honoré Mercier, the Liberal *nationaliste* who had won power by denouncing the murderers of Riel and who, some said, dreamt of an independent French Canadian state. His invitation to the premiers to attend an interprovincial conference at Québec – the first of many – found a ready response in Manitoba (locked in battle with Macdonald over the monopoly given to the CPR and a host of other western grievances), Nova Scotia (where an election had been fought and won on the cry of secession), New Brunswick, and Ontario (where Oliver Mowat had emerged as a determined and largely successful champion of provincial powers before the courts). Liberals all, thundered Macdonald, refusing to have anything to do with the Conference. But the stage had been set. The provinces would not accept his view of federation. The grand design was weakening and shimmying at the centre.

He also lived to hear many question the National Policy. The promised expansion had not come, and the late 1880s and early 90s were years of recession, unemployment, and emigration to greener pastures south. The Liberals had their answer – to reject the closed border policy and seek freer trade, reciprocity, even commercial union with the United States. To Macdonald, the Liberal nostrum was heresy, a treason worse than Riel's, for it would lead to the disappearance of the Canadian nation. Old and tired when the election campaign of 1891 began, he mustered all his strength and called up his cunning. "The old man, the old flag, the old policy," was the Conservative call, and of these perhaps "the old man" was the most critical. "The question which you will shortly be called upon to determine," he thundered from countless platforms across the land, "resolves itself into this. Shall we endanger our possession of the great heritage bequeathed to us by our fathers....with the prospect of ultimately becoming a portion of the American Union? As for myself, my course is clear. A British subject I was born, a British subject I will die. With my utmost effort, with my latest breath, will I oppose the 'veiled treason' which attempts by sordid means and mercenary offers to lure our people from our allegiance."

The old man, the old concertina player, brought the Conservatives their last victory for many years. He lay ill in bed as the results came in, and though he rallied briefly, two months later – on June 6, 1891 – Old Tomorrow was gone, universally mourned, and many a drink drunk to his name.

The Painting:

I had a strong impression of John A. Macdonald, the most important Prime Minister of all, because of his human frailties and his great vision – an idea as great as Washington's. He had flamboyance. His drinking, and stories connected to it, often seem humourous; in reality, they were tragic. In most portraits, I see sadness in his face. The good old days were not so good for Old Tomorrow. He must have had tremendous perseverance and courage. He must have been hard on himself. I was aware of pain and compassion.

The painting is the largest in the series, a triptych, a form I like. It is a painting of the whole country, in an abstract sense. I could have filled it with many images but I wanted the strength of simplicity, appropriate to symbolize Macdonald, who broke new ground with broad strokes. I see blue and white as the colours of Canada. These colours appear in several other paintings in the series and dominate a painting I did in 1970 called "The Canadian Dream." They

9

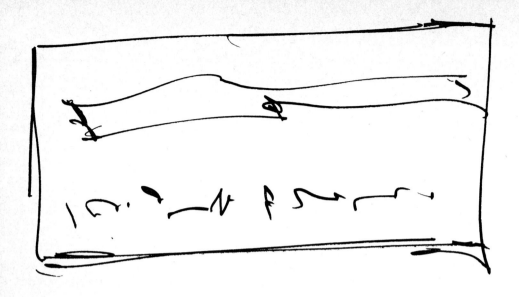

dominate this painting, too, in broad planes across the canvases. There is a lot of drawing underneath the painting, which is stretched by horizontal lines. At the middle, rising to one side, are reds and other colours emerging in turmoil. Outlines of structured forms in black rest at the base of the canvases. In the centre, a few lines indicate Macdonald's eyes and face, his continuing presence. It's as if he were embedded in the whole country, a giant we should celebrate. I find it ridiculous that we have not declared a holiday for him.

IF MACKENZIE had been blessed with a different name, he would not be forgotten, but there are many Mackenzies in our history: another Alexander, first to cross Canada by land; William Lyon Mackenzie, the Yonge Street rebel of 1837; and William Lyon Mackenzie King, whose portly ghost stalks the sepulchres of political life. But Alexander Mackenzie, Canada's first Liberal prime minister, deserves a better fate.

He was born poor in 1822 in Scotland and, as a young teenager, was apprenticed to a stone-mason. Coming to Canada at twenty with the family of his sweetheart, he became a successful builder in Kingston and Sarnia, where he also ran the Lambton Reformer, a staunchly Grit or Liberal paper. Many years later, when he was prime minister, Goldwin Smith said: "A stone-mason he was, and a stone-mason he still is." However unkind, there was truth in the observation. Mackenzie's spelling was uncertain, his grammar questionable, his speech flat, matter-of-fact and tied to the business at hand. He believed that hard work and sober habits led to success. Self-made, he had little sympathy for the less fortunate. A humble man, he was stiff-necked about class distinctions, and three times refused a knighthood. He was not a man of warmth or charm, being stubborn, uncompromising and self-righteous. Lacking great intellect or a good education, he distrusted both. Some men, he thought, were too clever by half, and such was Edward Blake, the brilliant Liberal lawyer who could have been, and should have been, the Liberal leader, but Blake's self-doubts and paranoia led him to brood rather than assume the burden. For five years, Blake moved in and out of Mackenzie's cabinet at will, equally stubborn, uncompromising, and self-righteous.

But if Mackenzie lacked talents, he possessed great industry. No Prime Minister has ever worked harder; he gave more time, John A. said, "than the country had the right to expect." Not only was he Prime Minister, but he became Minister of Public Works. He wanted to make sure the ministry was honest and efficient, serving the public rather than being a centre for political favouritism and corruption. He was in his office day and night, constantly lamenting that he was often the only minister to be found in Ottawa. He was as prudent with public money as he was with his own, and did not believe that "to the victor belongs the spoils." A specially constructed secret staircase let him escape patronage seekers who thronged his outer office.

Mackenzie thought Canadian political life was debased and needed his purifying Liberal principles. He introduced the secret ballot to protect voters from their own greed and the coercion of priests and factory owners. Simultaneous elections ended the nefarious practice of running sure winners first, stampeding the less certain who feared losing government patronage. Strict election expense controls, if they did not stamp out bribery, at least exposed the grafters.

He was also a nationalist and a democrat, and with Blake supplying the philosophic and legal content, he protested the Governor General's attempt to interfere in domestic affairs and insisted that any differences with Britain be settled by negotiation rather than the exercise of power by the Imperial appointee. As a further step along the road to Canadian autonomy, he created the Supreme Court of Canada and tried to make it the final court of appeal, but he was opposed by Macdonald and the British. He did not press the issue and the Judicial Committee of the Privy Council remained a final court of appeal until 1949.

But secret ballots and Supreme Courts and penny-pinching patronage are not the stuff of successful party leaders and Prime Ministers. Mackenzie's strict Liberal principles didn't prepare him for the great question of the day: the failure of the new Dominion to bring the economic prosperity it had promised. By 1873, the country was slipping into a severe cyclical depression that lasted until 1879. As a good nineteenth century Liberal, Mackenzie believed in free trade and sound finance, low taxes and a balanced budget. Soon after taking office, he sent George Brown, pre-eminent Liberal and owner-editor of the Toronto Globe, to Washington to negotiate a new reciprocity treaty that would open American markets, only to see the American Senate reject it out-of-hand. He did raise the tariff slightly to garner additional revenues, but when the Conservatives joined the manufacturers and farmers demanding increased protection against American goods, he refused to budge. A tariff, he protested, was simply a tax on 95 percent of the people for the benefit of the other five. He shared the sentiments of Richard Cartwright, his Minister of Finance, who refused to rob the public "on behalf of the poor and needy manufacturers who occupy those squalid hovels which adorn the suburbs of Montreal, Hamilton, and every city in the Dominion."

He also refused to risk the solvency of the country by pushing the Pacific Railway too far, too fast. No private company was willing to build the line during the depression, so Mackenzie built it in sections, linking the waterways through the Great Lakes. Macdonald had aimed the railway at the Rockies hoping a suitable pass would show up; the cautious Mackenzie believed the railway should inch across the west in step with settlement while surveyors found the best mountain pass and ocean terminal. It was not a policy that limbered up the imagination, but it was rational and certainly reflected the view that Ontario should not be too heavily taxed for a link with what Blake contemptuously called, "that sea of mountains."

As the 1878 election approached, Mackenzie faced a rejuvenated Macdonald stumping around the country with his National Policy promise to protect farmers and workers, manufacturers and financiers, his ringing declaration that, "There has risen in this country a CANADIAN PARTY which declares we must have Canada for the Canadians." Macdonald's charisma, Mackenzie's earnestness; it was no contest. It was a hard time for a man who only wanted to go home by the back stairs. Believing he had brought industry and honesty to government, safeguarding the public interest against rapacity and venality, he went to the polls certain that other men of perspicacity and prudence would support him. But he had not built up the Liberal party. He had neglected politics for administration, believing voters and the party poltroons would support the call for good management. (They never do, as Joe Clark found out.) As Grip, the humorous magazine, put it after the election: "He was always sitting, you remember, like a clerk: slaving, I may say, as he always would do, when it would have been better for the party had he been seeing people and wining, dining and poking bartenders in the ribs, jovially, like John A. But he could never be taught these little arts.... There was no gin and talk about MAC." Gin and talk and the National Policy swept Macdonald back into office in 1878, and Mackenzie into near oblivion.

Two years later, the party dumped him in favour of Edward Blake. Although partially paralyzed and his speech impaired by a stroke, Mackenzie remained in the Commons, a forlorn figure until his death in 1892.

The Painting:

I admire Mackenzie. He did his best with a job he never wanted. I admire him for his honesty and integrity. He shouldered a burden thrust on him by others. The painting has a solidity befitting a dour Scottish builder, but it also reflects the confusion, struggle and disappointment of his tenure. Two squares made up of blocks – one strong and solid, one barely visible – enclose a large white negative space. Within this structure, there is effort, worry, and anguish, the figure of a man striving, flailing the air, almost drowning, trying to get away. One of the interesting things about all these men, until I got to Laurier (and I painted him second-last), is that few of them moved me to great colour. Ordinarily my work is full of colour. I hadn't planned this at all. Many of the paintings are black and white, or blue and white, with colour added. This strange whiteness seems to haunt them. A critic, writing about me in The New Yorker, talked about the whites Canadians get in their paintings, how different we are from Americans: a stark white, perhaps the void... or perhaps it is the whiteness of the reluctant virgins who came to power in this country – from Mackenzie to Trudeau. In some of us, it is perhaps a sense of destiny sapped before begun, as if we were embedded in whiteness. The scale of the painting is justified by Mackenzie having been the first Liberal Prime Minister. He left a firm impression on me because of his high personal standards.

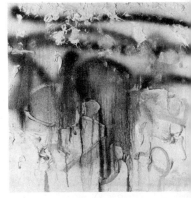

Working study: oil 20" × 20"
ALEXANDER MACKENZIE

S IR JOHN ABBOTT was seventy when fate dealt a hand he neither wanted nor deserved. A man who loathed politics, he was made Prime Minister: "I hate notoriety, public meetings, public speeches, caucuses and everything I know of the necessary incident of politics – except doing public work to the best of my ability." Macdonald, faced with racial and religious divisions and revelations of corruption, had been too busy trying to hold the party together to worry about a successor. As Abbott said, he was selected – accepted would be a better word – because he was not obnoxious to anyone. He was the man nobody wanted and everybody got. The obvious successor, and certainly the most able man in the cabinet, was John Thompson, but Thompson refused the Governor General's invitation to form a government. He feared a Catholic would not be accepted by the anti-Catholic faction in the party and country. Out of duty, and with little pleasure, Abbott accepted his thankless task. As a member of the Senate, however, he was at a disadvantage, and the real work of running the government and the country fell to Thompson, anyway, as he was made government leader in the House of Commons.

Abbott, born in Québec in 1821, was the first Canadian-born Prime Minister. Educated at McGill University, he became one of the colony's leading experts on commercial law, and at 34, Dean of the Law Faculty at McGill, a position he held until 1880. Like many Montréal businessmen, he had signed the Annexation Manifesto in 1849 when Britain had adopted free trade and given Canada responsible government – leaving Tories to an uncertain economic future and seemingly in the hands of reformers who had a belief in popular government. Like some Québec anglophones, he had opposed Confederation because he feared for the rights of an English minority in a province run by the French.

With the exception of the years 1874 to 1880, Abbott sat (or rested) in the legislature and the House of Commons, but his real work lay outside as counsel for a number of railways and ultimately, in 1880, as legal counsel for the new Canadian Pacific Railway, that consortium of Montréal capitalists given a western empire by Macdonald for throwing the line of steel across the continent. Abbott was rewarded for services to the CPR and Conservatives by an appointment to the Senate in 1887. Then, Macdonald made him government leader and a Minister without Portfolio in the cabinet. He became a caretaker Prime Minister for a year-and-half and once he was installed, wished he wasn't: "I should get on pretty well," he lamented, "if it were not for the deputations wanting money and the people wanting situations and plunder." He preferred whist to politics, and his Montréal clubs to the Parliament buildings, but as a most unlikely reluctant virgin he did his duty. A heart attack in August 1892, however, gave him his way out, and on doctor's advice, he quit work and resigned. Less than a year later, he was dead.

The Painting:

Sir John Abbott's life seemed disconnected, paradoxical. He signed the 1849 Annexation Manifesto, opposed Confederation, and was at the centre of the Pacific Scandal, and yet, he became Prime Minister in a nationalist government. He did not particularly want the job either. I felt he was strong-willed, something of a maverick, a formalized but free spirit. The painting is blue and white, and loose, but firmly contained within the square. Many abstractionists claim the square is the most human of forms. This is an expressionist painting with cubist elements, cubism often being the formalization of a free spirit, the rush of emotion seeking boundaries of security. There are several short vertical lines, all black, save for one red. There are no obvious links between the lines, as the connections between notes are only heard when hearing a whole piece of music. The silences between notes are the connections. Such unconnected lines can be used to describe a whole that is filled with contradictions. He was such a man. The loose, squiggly blue swirls are, I suppose, conflict and a turmoil firmly contained at the edges. Though not obvious, a rigid internal structure is laid against the free movement. All is superimposed on negative space. In terms of the rest of my work, I would never have produced such a painting if I had not been trying to capture the personalities of the Prime Ministers. It and others evolved out of structures and colours I seldom, if ever, put to use.

Working study: oil 20″ × 20″

SIR JOHN ABBOTT

I F THOMPSON hadn't died at fifty he might be remembered as one of our most distinguished Prime Ministers, or as a fine judge of the Supreme Court. Even so, his legal and political careers were remarkable. Few men of his age have been a provincial cabinet minister, a premier, a judge of the Nova Scotia Supreme Court, the federal Minister of Justice, and Prime Minister.

He was born in Halifax in 1844, the son of a civil servant of modest means, and remained a man of very modest means all his life. Called to the bar at 21, entry into politics was natural for he naturally, as an ambitious lawyer, went into politics (this relationship between the law – especially corporate as opposed to civil rights law – and power, is an extraordinary feature of our political life), and such was his ability that within a year of his election to the provincial legislature as a Conservative in 1877, he was made Attorney-General. He became Premier in 1882, but his government was defeated a few months later, and Thompson readily accepted an appointment to the bench. By 1885, Macdonald desperately needed new blood in his federal cabinet, particularly someone who might match the formidable debating talents of Blake and Wilfrid Laurier – the rising star of Liberalism. Thompson seemed such a man, and Macdonald asked him to become Minister of Justice. His initial reply sounded negative, but Sir John sensed otherwise: "Whispering, she would ne'er consent, consented," he joked to a colleague. "He is our man when we want him." And he was, in September of 1885, just in time to face the furor over the trial and execution of Riel.

In the House of Commons, he was a powerful presence. He carried the debates on the execution of Riel and the Jesuits Estates Act, which so inflamed Protestant Canada, with poise and fair-mindedness, hoping to cool the passions of racial and religious conflict. His speeches in the Commons were direct and forceful, his arguments those of a trained lawyer but not without political sensitivity, his mastery of the evidence always unquestioned. As historian Peter Waite wrote, Thompson operated in debate "the way a well-engineered warship, cleanly, efficiently, beautifully run would be brought to operate upon the enemy in war." The "great discovery of my life," said Sir John A. "was my discovery of Thompson."

Thompson was the obvious choice to succeed Macdonald, but Lady Macdonald felt he was right to refuse the Governor General's request: "There would have been, I am sure, a stampede of Ontario supporters. It is not so much his religion as the fact of being a pervert..." It was one thing in the 1890s to be born Catholic: to be born Protestant and convert to Catholicism for love, as Thompson had, was beyond the understanding or toleration of Protestant Ontario. But Thompson ran Abbott's government, and when the old man resigned there was really no other choice.

Thompson was short and usually overweight, fond of a good table, and preferred long hours with books to any physical exercise. He was amiable, but not one of the boys like Sir John A. Ambitious and with a very ambitious wife, he appeared almost indisposed to power, but privately he could be arrogant and was secretly contemptuous of many of his shallow, pretentious, deceitful colleagues. He also had a sharp tongue: "Blake came back last night and was 'awfully clever' for about half an hour," he wrote his wife, "& then went up on the back benches and picked his nose and cut his nails for the rest of the night." Lady Aberdeen, the wife of the Governor General, enjoyed Thompson's company, and respected his sincerity and integrity, his quiet sense of fun and usual good humour. "It was a delight to work with such a man," she confided to her Journal, "who was never so full of himself as to be afraid of his own prestige being diminished by giving due place & weight to the influence of the Governor General & who was always ready to talk everything over & to consider things from all points of view, whilst always having strong opinions of his own which he did not hesitate to express."

As Prime Minister, Thompson spent much of his time abroad, at the Intercolonial Conference in London dealing with copyright, and as the British representative at the Bering Sea arbitration in Paris. At home, the country was again mired in a sharp recession, following a short boom in the 80s, and Thompson hoped that the Colonial Economic Conference, which he hosted in Ottawa in 1894, might stimulate Canadian trade. But the issue that dominated political life was the Manitoba Schools question. By the time Thompson became Prime Minister, the courts had ruled that Manitoba had the power to abolish separate schools. The question, then, was whether the federal government would exercise its power to pass remedial legislation and restore separate schools. To French Canadians in the cabinet, it was a simple political decision, and they insisted the government act. But Thompson and his anglophone colleagues, who also knew it was a political decision but feared the consequences, argued the decision was really judicial, and once again delayed, asking the courts whether the federal government had, in fact, the power to coerce Manitoba. In a dubious decision, the Supreme Court ruled that Ottawa had no power to act. The Judicial Committee began to hear the appeal the day before Thompson died suddenly at the luncheon table at Windsor Castle on December 12, 1894.

As Lady Aberdeen wrote, it was "a black day indeed for Canada" and Laurier, then the Liberal leader, confessed that, "the death of poor Thompson is a most shocking event. It has strangely affected me. He was a gentleman & an able man, & there was genuine pleasure in a fight with him. Who is there now on the other side who can maintain the contest on the same level?"

The Painting

Thompson fascinated me. He converted to Catholicism at a time when some people called converts perverts. He came to the office young but as I've said, died before he could put his stamp on the country. It took two tries to get Thompson. He really excited me. The painting is the same size as "Tupper" but it has more movement. If his political life had not been cut short it would have been larger, an even stronger expressionistic painting. The vibrant, shooting col-

ours are diversity, his energies, the growth and promise that seemed inherent in him. As it gets muddier, I feel a blotting out of potentiality and opportunity, a life unfulfilled.

I worked out the space the way a figure painter might work with the body. There is the beginning of a border but it remains unfinished. The black looms like approaching death, the menace of mortality; it overpowers. When I paint with people in mind, names sometimes come through to me, and on to the canvas, as in this painting. Thompson had a raw talent and I felt a closeness to him. I experienced a genuine sadness when doing this painting. I'm surprised so few know anything about him.

"ERE WE ARE" George Foster, the cynical Conservative Minister of Finance said, "twelve of us, & every one of us as bad, or as good as the other." They were pondering their paltry future after Thompson's death. "Jack as good as his master," he added, and he was right. There was no leader among them. The great party had fallen upon unhappy days, racked by bitter rivalries and deep-seated religious and racial divisions that had bedevilled Canadian life since the 80s. But Mackenzie Bowell had been in the cabinet since 1878, his seniority recognized by selection as acting Prime Minister in Thompson's absence. And it was to Bowell that the Governor General, Lord Aberdeen, reluctantly looked in December 1894 (these years seemed rooted in reluctance). Perhaps no one could have saved the Conservative party from disaster, but Mackenzie Bowell was least likely of all.

He was a journeyman politician. Born in England in 1823, he and his parents settled in Belleville a decade later. His father worked as a carpenter. As a youth, he apprenticed as a printer's devil and came to edit and own the Belleville Intelligencer, an ardent Conservative paper. He joined the militia and saw service in the Fenian raids after the American civil war. As a young man, he also joined the Orange Order and wore the sash for life. The Order, banned in Britain – a sour, sullen stain of bigotry – was a citadel of uncompromising Protestanism and Imperial loyalty. For many years he was Grand Master of the Orange Association of British North America, but later and to his credit, as a politician he did not endorse the outrageous anti-Catholicism loose in Ontario. In 1867, he was returned as the Conservative member for North Hastings and represented the riding until Thompson sent him to the Senate in 1893.

Bowell was not stupid, but he was neither sharp nor quick. People found him evasive, and Lady Aberdeen complained that pinning him down was like nailing jelly to the wall. His evasiveness was not necessarily deceit, but a combination of weakness, indecision, old age, and an inability to grasp the point in a question. Totally out of his depth, Mackenzie Bowell was a man to be pitied, not condemned.

His colleagues never accepted him as leader, and from the day he took office until he resigned there were constant intrigues within the cabinet and open squabbles in the party. In January 1895, the Judicial Committee decided that the federal government had the power to intervene in the Manitoba Schools question but was not compelled to do so. It was, therefore, a political decision that had to be made. Cabinet and the party, however, were fatally divided. Macdonald had carpentered the Conservative Party out of apparently irreconcilable elements: French Canadian Catholics, many from the ultramontane and nationalistic wing—and anti-popery Orangemen, cemented by financial and commercial interests, all sheltered in the National Policy. After 1885, Macdonald had been unable to keep the party united and watched forlornly as some followers embarked on an anti-French and anti-Catholic crusade in Ontario. His Québec wing disintegrated. The Manitoba issue finally shattered the old alliance. Most Catholics demanded justice for the minority and many looked to the Québec bishops for moral and, ultimately, political support. Protestants demanded 'national' or secular schools, denouncing ecclesiastical interference in politics.

Although an Orangeman, Bowell agreed that an injustice had been done, and when it became clear that Manitoba would not obey an order to restore Catholic schools, the cabinet decided to introduce remedial legislation. But Bowell's shilly-shallying, his procrastination, his inability to fill cabinet positions, convinced seven of his ministers that, in the interests of the party, he should resign and make way for Sir Charles Tupper, the old War Horse of the party, then enjoying life as High Commissioner in London. The crisis –provoked by the "nest of traitors" – lasted for two weeks, until Bowell finally accepted Tupper as leader in the Commons. He also agreed to resign as soon as the session was over. But Tupper could not get the controversial bill through the Commons and, after replacing Bowell as Prime Minister on May 1, led the Conservatives to defeat in the June election.

Sir Mackenzie Bowell, duly knighted for next-to-nothing in 1895, never forgave the nest of traitors and probably never fully understood why they despised him. But he remained as government leader in the Senate until he resigned in 1906. He died in 1917, a few days short of his 94th birthday.

The Painting:

I did not have a redeeming sense of Sir Mackenzie Bowell. He was ambitious, argumentative, a staunch Orangeman of limited ability, the least impressive of the Prime Ministers. He did, however, decide to order Manitoba to re-instate sectarian schools. Though he dithered, that decision showed resolve and courage. I tried three times to capture Bowell. The painting does not have strong, vibrant colours. It was quite bright until toned down with a light layer of white. There is a lot of underpainting on the canvas and some of the colour still comes through, diluted. Movement is firmly contained within the square. In the context of the series, the Bowell is small. I could not bring myself to make it bigger. He was not cut out for the job. He was, however, a Prime Minister and as a painting it stands with the rest.

Working study: oil 20" × 20"
SIR MACKENZIE BOWELL

S IR CHARLES TUPPER was Prime Minister for sixty-eight days, but he was one of the giants of post-Confederation Canada. Born in Nova Scotia in 1821, he graduated in medicine from Edinburgh at 22 and had a good practice. Entering politics in 1855 with a remarkable victory over Joseph Howe, the tribune of Nova Scotia, he soon became a member of the cabinet and by 1864 was Premier. Tupper played an important role at the Québec and Charlottetown conferences, and skilfully brought Nova Scotia, bawling and kicking, into Confederation. But opposition to union with Canada was so deep that of the seventeen members elected to Ottawa, Tupper alone supported Confederation.

From 1867 to 1884, Tupper sat in the Commons, becoming Macdonald's right-hand man. He was the key designer of the National Policy before the 1878 election and as the Minister of Railways, was responsible for the Canadian Pacific. Macdonald sent him to London as High Commissioner in 1884, but when thorns came up in the political thickets in 1887 – and there was another critical election – he brought him back temporarily as the Minister of Finance. After Macdonald's death, Tupper watched from London as the drama unfolded; a man always in the wings, he waited patiently for the call and when it became clear Bowell would have to go, Tupper found it convenient to return to Canada where he received the reins so reluctantly handed over.

Sir Charles' task was to get the remedial bill, forcing Manitoba to restore separate schools, through the House of Commons. But the 112 clauses in the bill gave the Liberals and Conservative rebels ample opportunity to obstruct. Sessions were long, the discussions mean and the scenes unedifying as strong drink kept members awake and sometimes, it would appear from the debates, on their feet. There was little Tupper could do, for the introduction of closure lay in the future, in the mind of Arthur Meighen. After a month's debate, only fifteen of the clauses had passed and with the five-year life of parliament about to expire, Tupper adjourned the debate, dissolved parliament and faced the people. Their verdict was clear: after five years of disintegration, decay, and distrust in English and French Canada, and with the country still mired in the recession, the time had come for change.

However skilful with forceps or scalpel, Dr. Tupper the politician swung a club. On the hustings or in the Commons, he was rough and feisty. He lacked Macdonald's easy good humour and ability to banter, Thompson's capacity to marshall an argument, and was "a parliamentary bully boy who could be depended upon to defend anything or oppose anything the party interest (or Tupper's) required to be defended or opposed." But he had courage and a blustery kind of charisma. He was audacious in his free and easy way with facts and his frequent propositioning of secretaries.

After his defeat, Sir Charles remained leader of the opposition until 1901, when he retired from public life. He died in England on October 30, 1915, a month after his 94th birthday. His death was front-page news in Canada.

The Painting:

I had difficulty with Tupper. In the beginning, I had a faint impression of him and the first oil sketch had an expansive and visionary sense but lacked boldness and solidity. I found these virtues when I looked at him again. I saw a strong leader who was full of brass, a fighter, but also a man of ideas and skill who gave long and important service to our political life.

The painting began with solid blocks of red, white and blue, but other strong colours eased into it naturally. At first, there was a black border but this changed to crimson, eliminating a flatness, making it bolder and stronger, befitting the Warhorse from Cumberland. There is a brazen air and building-block strength to the canvas but also formal ritual. With Tupper, I realized that the difficult thing was to not make these paintings illustrative, and yet to let subcon-

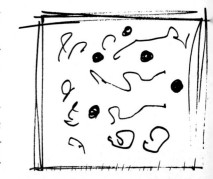

scious symbols or even obvious symbols appear, without sticking them in the eye of the viewer.

Though smaller in context, the painting is a substantial size. I was pleased that Tupper became Prime Minister just short of his seventy-fifth birthday and lived to be ninety-three. Today – when life is longer – we worry that our leaders are sixty-five or seventy. We forget that it takes time for shrewd whippersnappers to become wise Warhorses.

Working study: oil 20″ × 20″

SIR CHARLES TUPPER

L AURIER, frail all his life, a tall and elegant figure always nattily dressed, said what he intended to do: "My object is to consolidate Confederation, and to bring our people long estranged from each other gradually to become a nation. This is the supreme issue. Everything else is subordinate to that idea." This was not the rhetoric of a calculating politician. It was the principle by which Sir Wilfrid Laurier lived. He was also, of course, a calculating politician.

As Macdonald had given Canada its body, so Laurier was to try to find its soul. He struggled to find some semblance of Canadian unity at the core of racial, religious and regional divisions, and at the core of Canada's relations with Great Britain, which often threatened any internal accord, as the country moved, often unwittingly, from colony to nation. That's what he tried to do. Tragically, as leader of the Liberal Party for thirty-two years and Prime Minister for fifteen, he saw Canada more deeply divided than ever before.

Laurier was ideally equipped for national reunification. He was the first – and until Pierre Trudeau – the only Prime Minister almost equally at home in two languages and cultures. Born in St. Lin, a little village thirty miles north of Montréal, he was sent to board with an English family when he was eleven. From L'Assomption College he went to McGill University, where he became familiar with the principles of British law, the classics of British political theory, and the broad sweep of British history. Soon after graduation, he moved to L'Avenir where, after briefly editing a rouge newspaper, he acquired a modest law practice. In 1871, he entered the provincial assembly as a Liberal, and three years later was elected to the House of Commons where he remained for the rest of his life.

The future seemed bleak for Québec Liberals in the 1870s. The old rouge, from whom the Liberals were descended, had been outspokenly anti-clerical, sometimes republican, guilty of that form of Catholic Liberalism denounced by the Pope in the 1864 Syllabus of Errors, holding the mistaken belief "that the Roman Pontiff can and ought to reconcile himself to, and agree with, progress, liberalism and civilization." And, for the benefit of a less sophisticated audience, the Québec bishops elaborated on the Syllabus, denouncing Liberalism as "a snake which wriggles into all ranks of Christian society, and steals even into the sanctuary, to spread trouble and desolation." The Church, from bishop to priest, openly engaged in electioneering, using denial of the sacraments as a weapon against those who did not know that voting Liberal was a sin.

It took courage to be a Liberal, like Laurier's father, and young Laurier found the situation intolerable. He hated bigotry, distrusted any arbitrary authority. Believing in democracy and the right of the individual to live by his conscience, regardless of his faith, he could not tolerate this exercise of ecclesiastical power. To an Ontario friend who urged him to join Mackenzie's cabinet, Laurier wrote: "From that moment my quietness & my happiness will be gone. It will be a war with the clergy, a war of every day, of every moment, with the most ignorant, the most bitter, the most prejudiced foes that man ever had to contend with. I will be denounced as Antichrist. You may laugh at that, but it is no laughing matter with us."

Two years later, in June 1877, Laurier displayed his courage and gambled his political future with a sensational public speech on Liberalism which was an open assault on the church. Québec Liberals, he argued, no longer found their roots in the radical Liberalism of continental Europe, but in the evolutionary and democratic Liberalism of Great Britain. Parties in Canada could not be distinguished morally, he continued, and while the priest might say "that if I am elected, the State will be endangered," he could not use his religious authority to intimidate the voter. For then parties would be religious and not political. There were those, bishops and laymen, who wished to see a political party based on Catholic principles. But, he asked, "have you not reflected that by that very fact you will organize the Protestant population as a single party, and then, instead of the peace and harmony now prevailing between the different elements of the Canadian population, you will throw open the doors to a war, a religious war, the most terrible of all wars?"

Laurier's speech outraged the bishops, but the gamble paid off.

Rome sent instructions that the Church could not "teach from the pulpit that it was a sin to vote for any particular candidate or party, even more it is forbidden to announce you will refuse the sacraments for this cause." Now that he was the rising star of Liberalism, Laurier could write that clerical influence can be met and fought: "It cannot be overcome, but it is a great advantage to be able to say to conscientious and intelligent Catholics that by the authority of the Pope they are free."

Soon afterwards, Laurier entered the Mackenzie cabinet, and under Blake was recognized as the Liberal leader in Québec, a province inflamed by Honoré Mercier's cry, "Riel, our bother is dead, victim of fanaticism and treason." Laurier's less dramatic, "Had I been on the banks of the Saskatchewan I would myself have shouldered a musket," was thrown back at him for decades, but his critics forgot this musket would have been shouldered in defence of constitutional rights, for had the government "taken as much pains to do right, as they have taken to punish wrong, they would never have had any occasion to convince those people that the law can be violated with impunity, because the law would never have been violated at all."

Laurier's steady performance in the Commons, his quiet winning ways among his colleagues, and the promise of growing support in Québec, led Blake to select Laurier as his successor in 1887. Laurier accepted with grave misgiving, for he believed that English Canada would never accept a French Canadian Catholic as Prime Minister – a view shared by many English Canadians. And there were many others, Liberals included, who endorsed the view of the Tory Montreal Gazette: "Wanting in training, the knowledge and industry indispensable in the occupant of such a position, he is, however, a kindly genial gentleman, courteous in manner, and will make a very good figurehead for a weak and incohesive party." Nine years later the figurehead was Prime Minister.

After the 1891 defeat on unrestricted reciprocity, Laurier abandoned free trade and accepted protection, thus making it possible for businessmen to support the party. As the Québec Conservatives disintegrated, moderates swung towards the Liberals. And strong

Liberal governments in most provinces added their support to the national party. But the Manitoba Schools question threatened to shatter their superficial unity. For six years, Laurier refused to state his policy, confessing he was not courageous but "to exhibit the spectacle of a divided opposition would have been simply playing the game of the government." By 1895, he was only prepared to recall the fable of the man who had shed his coat for the sun, not the wind: "If it were in my power, I would try the sunny way." In the 1896 election, Québec Liberals promised Laurier's sunny way would persuade Manitoba to restore separate schools, and despite the bishops' open support for the Conservatives, Québec went Liberal. Elsewhere, the election was a draw, the electorate weighing suspicion of a French Canadian leader against the spectacle of a discredited and divided Tory party.

Historians Ramsay Cook and Craig Brown have said this about the first French Canadian Prime Minister: "At fifty-five he was near the height of his powers in 1896. Balding at the front, his hair – not yet the silver plumage of later years – flowed back fashionably to touch his high Victorian collar. Frock-coated suits and double-breasted vests set him off stylishly, even somewhat romantically. And he wore a top hat, and sometimes a cloth cap, with elegance. His strong, distinctive face broke easily into a smile when he greeted a political friend, and even when he skilfully admonished an erring foe. A friendly, if carefully controlled personality, he attracted genuine affection from adulators and critics alike. It was his deep-set eyes, perhaps, that best revealed the will and determination that were an important part of this politician's make-up."

Laurier was an artist in politics, and the sheer artistry of the performance masked the will of a man as tough and determined as Macdonald, whom he had watched for so long and from whom he had learned so much. He was fluent in French and English: elegant in language as in dress, lofty in content, logical in argument, and moving in spirit. In public and in private, he radiated charm, and as Chubby Power, the hard-drinking Irishman from Québec City, said: "He had the gift of being loved," a sentiment endorsed by Henri Bourassa, who confessed that, "although I fought him because of

differences of principle, I loved him all my life and he knew that."
But for all his warmth, his charm, his love, he was, as one colleague
came to realize, "a masterful man set on having his way, and equally
resolute that his colleagues shall not have their way unless that is
quite agreeable to him."

Like Macdonald, Laurier had learned to take men as they were,
"and not such as you would like them to be." He realized that the
party was the instrument for gaining and keeping power, and he
played it beautifully. His idealism was curbed by his pragmatism.
"Reforms are for Oppositions," he remarked (and it's too bad he
couldn't have had a talk with Joe Clark), for "it is the business of
government to stay in power." Less cynically or realistically, he
admonished one critic with the observation that, "In politics, the
question seldom arises to do the ideal right. The best that is generally
to be expected is to attain a certain object, and for the accomplishment
of this object, many things have to be done which are questionable,
and many things have to be submitted to which, if rigorously
investigated, could not be approved of."

Laurier could be decisive and ruthless, but above all, he believed
in the art of persuasion and compromise, and there was some truth
in Bourassa's comment that the first thing he would do on reaching
the gates of Paradise would be to propose an honourable compromise between God and the Devil. Compromise was the key to the
unity of a sharply divided nation. "Our existence as a nation is the
most anomalous as has yet existed," he lectured a critic of his
continual compromising. "We are British subjects but we are an
autonomous nation; we are divided into provinces, we are divided
into races, and out of these confused elements the man at the head of
affairs has to sail the ship onwards, and to do this safely is not
always the ideal policy from the point of view of pure idealism which
ought to prevail, but the policy which can appeal on the whole to all
sections of the country." To Laurier, this was more than a political
calculus, it was the key to national unity, the supreme issue.

Laurier was fortunate in coming to power just as the lengthy
recession was coming to an end. There was no more free land on the

American frontier and the worldwide recovery brought the Canadian west into the world economy, and a million immigrants headed to the last, best west. In northern Ontario and Quebec, in the mountains of British Columbia, the rock was dotted with new mines and smelters, logging camps and pulp and paper towns, and the rivers yielded their raw power and new hydro-electric plants fed the factories and cities of an emerging industrial nation. Sheltered by the protective tariff, Canadian industries expanded and American branch plants leaped the border to serve a market that almost doubled in size between 1891 and 1914. So great was the optimism that not one but two transcontinental railways were flung across the country. The twentieth century, Laurier boasted, would belong to Canada.

But material prosperity alone could not bring national unity. Laurier had been able to negotiate a compromise on the schools question – one which, like all compromises, completely satisfied no one. But no sooner was the Manitoba situation resolved than Canada's relations with Britain posed a new threat to national unity. English Canadians shared the enthusiasm for empire that infected Victoria's England in the waning years of the century, finding expression in Kipling's verse and Joseph Chamberlain's attempt to create some kind of imperial federation. But French Canada could not share the enthusiasm for an empire which gloried in the supremacy of the Anglo-Saxon race and the necessary subjugation of lesser breeds beneath the law.

Laurier admired British institutions, and could speak glowingly of the Empire, but at heart he was a Canadian nationalist, and at successive Imperial Conferences, his rhetoric was more than matched by his refusal to make any commitments: "That damned dancing-master bitched the whole show," the Cape Colony Premier exploded to Kipling, and as one shrewd British observer wrote, Laurier seemed to prefer, "the present dependent Colonial position with the prospect of future separation to a position of national equality with the United Kingdom which would involve closer union between the different parts of the empire." True. Laurier did not believe in national equality within the Empire because he knew that it was impossible, and for Canada at least, undesirable. He was not a separatist. He was willing to wait.

The Boer War in 1899 revealed the dangers in the Imperial connection. English Canada was determined to participate in the South African war, to move from the vicarious pleasures of armchair imperialism and march to bugle and pipe. Almost to a man, French Canada was opposed. In the end, the sheer political power of the majority forced Laurier to send an army of volunteers, as Henri Bourassa resigned his seat in the Commons in protest. The seed was planted: in Québec, Laurier's compromises were perceived as French Canadian defeats.

The Imperial connection became increasingly critical as the First War approached, and a beleaguered Britain sought colonial assistance in matching the growing might of the German navy. The Conservatives, loyal to the core, demanded that Canada pay for the construction of some battleships. Laurier countered with a proposal to build a Canadian navy which, if the Empire was ever truly in danger, would be found at Britain's side. Conservatives denounced Laurier as a traitor to the Empire, a vacillating leader bowing to the dictates of Québec. Bourassa saw the tin pot navy as a clear commitment to fight at Britain's side, and final proof that Laurier could not be trusted with the destiny of French Canada.

The naval question surfaced just as Laurier was moving towards a dramatic change in Canadian trade policy. The prosperity of the boom years had not been evenly distributed. Farmers and other basic producers complained of the high cost of manufactured goods, and the difficulties of entering the American market. The Americans, too, for the first time in decades, were willing to talk reciprocity. And in 1911, a treaty was negotiated which allowed for free or freer trade in most natural products, and very few manufactured goods. The Conservatives were stunned. But the opposition soon emerged. Financiers, industrialists, merchants – the men who ran the banks, and Eaton's and Simpson's, and the railways – cloaking their economic interests behind the mask of patriotism – denounced the agreement as certain to lead not only to economic ruin but to political annexation. The Conservatives picked up the cry. Reciprocity was treason – Laurier a traitor – trading the independence of his country for a mess of Yankee pottage.

Laurier faced the people in 1911, calling out, "Follow my white plume." The results were disastrous. His party was obliterated in Ontario and lost heavily throughout English-speaking Canada. In Québec, the dissident Liberals, led by Bourassa, were joined by French Conservatives in their opposition to the naval bill, and Laurier's support fell sharply. Despondent and disillusioned, Laurier reflected on his defeat. "I am branded in Québec as a traitor to the French, and in Ontario as a traitor to the English. In Québec I am branded as Jingo, and in Ontario as a separatist. In Québec I am attacked as an Imperialist, and in Ontario as an anti-Imperialist. I am neither, I am a Canadian."

Laurier remained Liberal leader until his death in 1919. He supported Canada's participation in the war, and repeatedly urged his countrymen to enlist. But when the government determined upon conscription, he reluctantly but firmly refused to join a coalition conscription government and opposed the policy. Although his party split, as many Liberals supported conscription, Laurier felt he had no choice. To support conscription would place the province of Québec completely under the control of Bourassa and the nationalists. There would then have been little possibility of any post-war reconciliation. The objective of national unity, never more distant, it seemed, than in 1917 when the election showed how completely the English and French were divided, would then, perhaps permanently, be unrealizable. Laurier died on February 17, 1919, hopeful perhaps, but uncertain whether his Liberal party could once again become the instrument to forge national and international policies that could "bring our people long estranged from each other, gradually to become a nation."

The Painting:

I made three attempts at Laurier. I had an image of elegance and eloquence. With red, black, white and middle-gray in mind, I did sketches of long, narrow canvases, different paintings stacked against a wall. Laurier's elegance and order overpowered this too-fragmented effect: the painting needed to be more organized, unified, reflecting his sense of purpose. That gave way to a circle and Maltese cross, a static cross, too stilted in effect. Then, the final inspiration came from a sixteenth century Japanese screen called Early Spring.

The portrait is monumental, a portrait of birth – a planet or organic substance – lush with green and gold. It began as a busier painting, but I kept simplifying to give it strength and unity. There is only a little hot pink, made with crimson and white – rouge, if you will – left from those early experiments. The Maltese cross, large in the earlier versions, is still important but it has been diminished, as Laurier diminished the power of the Bishops. The green, a colour I have not used much in my palette, spreads across the canvases, giving breadth and scope, a larger sense.

There is a square within the centre panel, a formalization, a touch of propriety, like a table setting. I saw Laurier as a dapper Victorian gentleman, who had a known mistress. He was a good dancer, a good looking man.

The centre circular motion is tumultuous and has to do with the formation of the country. In my mind, it was like the formation of a planet; massive undercurrents merging together with great forces. There is darkness, too, marking the struggles of his final years.

I intended the frame to be an integral part of the painting, like architecture, as Laurier was a national figure in the fullest sense, a unifier and builder.

PRIME MINISTER for almost a decade, but Robert Borden remains a fuzzy, almost forgotten figure in our history. The First War, conscription, dominion autonomy, these are the events associated with his career. But Borden, who knew the classic languages, chewed tobacco and sometimes bicycled to work, remains as aloof from us as he was from his contemporaries.

He was born in the tiny Nova Scotia village of Grand Pré, in 1854, son of an Annapolis Valley farmer. His character was shaped by his mother, a strong-willed, intelligent and energetic woman who instilled in the young boy a strict moral code, a sometimes overwhelming commitment to duty, and a driving ambition to succeed. He was an excellent student, not only in mathematics and English, but in Latin and Greek. At fifteen, he became a teacher, but found the students disinterested and boring and teaching seemed no highway to fame and fortune. At twenty, he turned to law, standing first in the bar examinations, and before he was thirty, he had become a junior partner in a leading Halifax law firm. In the depressed 1890s, he was earning $30,000 a year, and wise investments in property, mortgages, stocks and bonds, had made him a wealthy man.

Borden was associated with the Tuppers, and in 1896 the old man persuaded him to run in Halifax, arguing that it could only help his law practice and that he need only stay for one term. Elected easily, Borden spent four disillusioning years in Ottawa, where he found the rich resources of the Library more congenial than debates in the House – and it was also a convenient escape from his relentless constituents. But he ran again, and in 1901, the Tuppers persuaded Borden to accept the leadership when old Sir Charles retired and forced Borden on a reluctant caucus.

Through the next decade, he tried to fashion a platform for the party. As usual, he worked alone. He was not a philosopher, a theorist, but a man of affairs interested in getting the job done. He believed in efficiency, good management, and approached public issues as a lawyer did a case. He was offended by the corruption in politics and business during the potlach of the boom years. The cause, he believed, "lies in a lack of moral earnestness, in the absence of a sense of individual responsibility, and in a certain spirit of soul-less commercialism, which has attended modern industrial development," and there would be no permanent remedy, he said, until "the individual citizen realizes and accepts his duty to the state." But government could help: appointments to the civil service based on merit and not political patronage; a cleaner political life if it were a criminal offence for corporations to make political donations "unless it is made public and unless the people thoroughly understand the amount of the contribution and the purpose for which it was devoted." To Borden, the State was not an innocent bystander, but an active player, functionally not ideologically, which should intervene to control public utilities, regulate economic activity, and own and manage railways and telephones. The tariff should be in the hands of an independent commission that would be concerned not only with the interests of the manufacturers but with those of the consumers. As he watched the rapid and wasteful exploitation of the country's natural resources and the emergence of huge new financial and industrial organizations, he warned that, "the vast accumulation of wealth in the hands of a few men confronts us with the possibility that great natural resources may pass into the hands of an oligarchy of wealth and may be used for the oppression rather than for the benefit of the people."

It was not an appealing philosophy to the Tory war lords of Montréal or Toronto, nor did his call for purity in politics appeal to the rank and file thirsting for its reward whenever Laurier might be defeated. There were constant rumblings within the party, and attempts to dump him failed only because there was no obvious alternative.

But fortune smiled in 1911 when the combination of the naval bill and Reciprocity, the arthritis of old age and the smell of scandal, fatally weakened the Laurier Liberals. Borden had long campaigned against Liberal corruption, and soon could shout "No truck nor trade with the Yankees" with the rest. In Québec, he readily allowed his French Canadian wing, under Frederick Monk, to adopt a policy opposed to his own on the naval question, and even funnelled Conservative funds to aid Bourassa and the Nationalists. Politics breeds awkward bedfellows, and none have been more ideologically promiscuous than the Liberal-Tory-big business-nationalist-imperialist group that bedded down in 1911.

The new Prime Minister, who suffered from insomnia, stomach problems, carbuncles and rheumatism in the neck, was not a politician. As he sat in the House, sometimes with a nurse standing close to massage his neck, he disliked the seamy side of politics, disliked public speaking, and found it physically and emotionally exhausting. He had a thinly disguised contempt for most people in politics, including his own supporters, and as leader and Prime Minister called caucus as seldom as possible, and when he did, was determined to get his own way. He had few close friends or trusted advisors in the party, or even in his cabinets, and often looked to friends outside for advice. To friends he was warm and affable, but to others he was cold and distant. He was not a man to "wink hard": he lacked the conviviality of a Macdonald, the personal charm of Laurier. He perhaps inspired a grudging respect, but not love. Throughout his career, he remained detached, a man who seemed to prefer golf, his books and bridge to the game of politics. Overwork made him irritable, impatient – and, hypochondriac by nature – a grumbler about his health. He enjoyed the exercise of power, but he seems always to have resented and hated the price he had to pay. Once in office, he found his party was unwilling to forego patronage, and it was not until after the War that he was able to establish a federal civil service based largely on merit. But the approach of war diverted attention from domestic matters, and Borden was never able to reveal how committed he was to the principle of state intervention. The naval question, in particular, demanded his immediate attention. Convinced that the German threat was real, he offered the British $35 million for new battleships. Monk resigned from the cabinet. Opposition in the Commons was only overcome by the invention of closure. A Liberal-dominated

Senate unceremoniously threw out the bill, and by 1914 nothing had been done.

Canada was automatically at war when Britain declared war, but the decision to go all out was Canada's. A War Measures Act gave the federal government total control over all aspects of Canadian life, and created what has been called a "democratic dictatorship." Within two months, 30,000 men of the First Division reached England and by February were in the front lines in France. Three other divisions followed, and the reputation of the Canadians as crack assault troops – the Somme, Ypres, Passchendaele, Hill 70 – was reflected in enormous casualties. Over 650,000 men and women served in the armed forces. Over 60,000 – or more than one in ten who saw active service – died, and more than one in three was wounded.

By the spring of 1917, following a trip to England, Borden was convinced that only conscription could provide the necessary reinforcements at the front. But he knew, also, that conscription was violently opposed in Québec, where even a rumour set off riots in the streets of Montréal. He first offered Laurier equal seats in a Union government, and when that failed, was able to bring a number of prominent Liberals into a government committed to conscription. But there was an election to win, and to make victory certain, Borden passed the Military Service Act which gave the vote to all the military and the Wartime Elections Act which gave the vote to all close female relatives of servicemen – and took it away from all post-1902 immigrants from enemy countries. And just before the election, the government appeased the farmers by exempting all farm labourers from compulsory service. The result was a foregone conclusion. Borden won only three English-speaking seats in Québec, as Laurier received almost 100 percent of the French Canadian vote. Outside Québec, the Liberals won only 29 seats, as English-speaking Canada gave 70 percent of its support to the Union government. There were some in Québec who spoke of separation, and on Easter Monday, 1918, in Québec City, an anti-conscription riot was ended only after troops were sent in and four killed and more than fifty wounded. In the end, 120,000 men were conscripted, and 47,000 were sent overseas. The price had been high, but in early 1918 no one knew that the war would be over in November.

Borden believed in conscription because he was a Canadian nationalist who saw Canada's all-out war effort as evidence of the move from colony to nation. Early in the war, he successfully demanded that the Canadian corps have a Canadian commander, and by 1916, insisted that Canada have some voice in the determination of war policy. "It can hardly be expected," he warned the British, "that we should put 400,000 or 500,000 men in the field and willingly accept the position of having no more voice than if we were toy automata. Any person cherishing such an expectation harbours an unfortunate and even dangerous delusion." The creation of an Imperial War Cabinet where the Dominion Prime Ministers could, on occasion, express their views, satisfied Borden for the moment. But in 1917, he played the leading role in forcing the British to agree that after the War there would be "a readjustment of constitutional relations" which would be based "upon a full recognition of the Dominions as autonomous nations of an Imperial Commonwealth," and would recognize their right "to an adequate voice in foreign policy and foreign relations...." It was a giant step, although, as it turned out, not in the direction the modern Commonwealth was to take. At the same time, Borden overcame British, French and American objections and signed the peace treaty and sat in the League of Nations as an independent state. Through dogged persistence, Borden had won for Canada a new place in the Empire and the world.

At home, post-war Canada was ravaged by conflicts of a different sort. The end of war brought severe dislocations: veterans looked vainly for jobs and homes, workers demanded long delayed wage increases, farmers pursued their own interests through a new political movement. The Bolshevik Revolution appealed to radicals, and the Red Scare terrified the middle class. Strikes were endemic, and in Winnipeg, a general strike paralyzed the city for weeks, threatening to spread across the country, and ended in violence and bloodshed.

Exhausted in body and spirit, Borden accepted his doctor's advice and after a lengthy absence from Ottawa, resigned in the summer of 1920, when the party elected Arthur Meighen to replace him. Sir Robert retired to the quiet of his study where he wrote learned essays on the constitution, prepared his memoirs, and penned long reflections on the state of the nation. He died in Ottawa on June 10, 1937.

The Painting:

Working study: oil 15″ × 12″

SIR ROBERT BORDEN

I had no idea what I was going to do with Borden. I had a sense of Borden as a jock, a big, tough guy, but in fact, he was given to dropping Latin phrases, chewing tobacco, reciting poetry. He was a

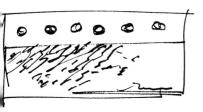

calm, contemplative man who hated militarism but had to lead his country into war. Ill, and suffering pain, he persevered, and I came to like him more and more. His qualities led me to think of horizontal movement. Paul Klee spoke of direction, lines and meaning. The horizontal line creates repose and quiet strength. The centre blue panel is painted with a polyester emulsion and acrylic paint which, when blended, creates chemical eruptions. The surface is heavily textured, even rough, and most of the crimson is painted out leaving a dominant blue. It is both serene and volatile, as was his life. The white space makes it float but the white is not perfect. There are lines which mar the surface; it couldn't be pristine, or anything suggesting sterility. The painting is a beautiful series of accidents which I hope capture the philosophical quality of the man, his strength, the tumult of his tenure. I would like to have known Borden. I believe I would have liked him.

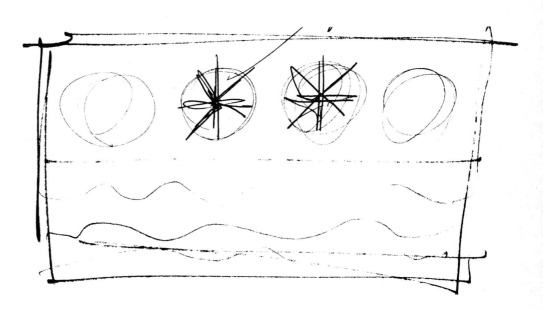

A FTER THE FIRST WAR peace brought enormous dislocation to the country. Farmers deserted the old parties to create their own. Labour was restless, sometimes violent, determined to find some political expression. French and English were deeply divided, Québec isolated, defensive, apprehensive. The times called for tolerance, patience, compromise – for men such as Laurier and Macdonald, honest brokers who might find some national concensus. But Sir Robert Borden's successor hardly seemed the man. As one shrewd journalist said, Arthur Meighen was "a fine parliamentarian and first class political advocate, but still regards all Liberals as children of the devil and has too hard and unyielding a mind for the times in which we live." Meighen himself was even more revealing: "This continual bending of the knee to local notions and prejudices is nothing but weak and foolish humbug and gets no person anywhere. The only unpardonable sin in politics is lack of courage. Indecision or doubt about a course once entered upon is inevitably fatal." Meighen had courage, and seldom was troubled by indecision or doubt. Courage to devise the strategy to win the 1917 election, using closure to get the bill through the Commons; courage to devise a way to take over the Canadian National Railway; courage to intervene ruthlessly in the Winnipeg General Strike; and courage to add section 98 to the Criminal Code, giving unlawful associations a definition broad enough to include almost any criticism of the established order. His courage earned him respect, but also made enemies.

Arthur Meighen was born in 1874 on a farm in Perth county, Ontario. A brilliant mathematics student at the University of Toronto, he was equally brilliant when he turned to law. Like so many other professionals, he moved west during the great boom to establish a law practice in Portage la Prairie, and like so many lawyers soon went into politics. Elected to the House of Commons as a Conservative in 1908, he at once gained a reputation as a skilful debater. In 1913, Borden made him Solicitor General and after the

War, a member of the cabinet and the man most responsible for managing Parliament, a role in which he demonstrated superbly his courage. When Borden resigned, Meighen had the support of the rank and file but not of his colleagues in the cabinet; but when their favourite refused, Meighen became leader and Prime Minister in July, 1920.

The new Prime Minister had a brilliant mind, cutting like a laser to the core of a question or to the weakness of an opponent's argument. He was ruthless in debate, asking no quarter and giving none, and his sharp tongue often offended friends as well as foes. He was coldly logical, and in public at least, lacked warmth and compassion. He faced the voters in December, 1921, without apologies for the past – to French Canada, to labour, to the immigrants whose votes he had taken away, and to the farmers whose desire for free trade he ridiculed as an "evangel which was to emancipate mankind and bring the light and glory of Heaven to the earth." Meighen believed in the tariff as firmly as Macdonald, and no amount of pressure from his more politically astute friends could make him soften his stand.

The result was a disaster. Meighen and the Conservatives won only 50 seats and the smallest popular vote in the party's history. The Liberals, under their new leader, Mackenzie King, won every seat in Québec, while the farmer's party, the Progressives, swept rural Ontario and the west to win 65 seats. Meighen resigned, and Mackenzie King began four years of sound, if unspectacular, government. In opposition, Meighen revealed another of his firm unshakeable convictions: that Canada's future was best assured as a member of an Imperial Commonwealth, an alliance of equals, where Canada would be a partner and play an ever increasing role in world affairs. Thus, when Mackenzie King rejected a British request for aid during a crisis in the middle east, Meighen thundered that the Canadian response should have been – "Ready, Aye Ready: we stand by you." It was not likely to win friends in Québec or the west.

But his enthusiasm for the Empire and his support of a protective tariff did win him support in Ontario and the Maritimes, and in the election of 1925, Meighen emerged with 117 seats, while King won only 101 and the Progressives fell to 24. King chose to face

Parliament rather than resign, but early in the 1926 session the revelation of serious corruption in the customs department lost the support of the Progressives. To avoid defeat, King asked the Governor General, Lord Byng, to dissolve Parliament. Thus began what generations of students and journalists have called the "King-Byng-Wing-Ding."

Lord Byng properly refused King's request. He believed that King, quite clearly defeated in 1925, should have resigned and allowed him to call on Arthur Meighen, leader of the largest party, to form a government. He had made it clear to King that he could not automatically expect a dissolution. After several heated arguments, with Byng refusing to budge or to seek instructions from London, King resigned. Byng then asked Meighen to form a new government. Meighen was hesitant, but after consulting Sir Robert Borden, he agreed, feeling, some say, that it was his duty, and anxious, others say, to grasp the reins of power once again.

At that time, it was necessary for new cabinet ministers to resign their seats and seek re-election. Meighen did resign, and watched the proceedings in the House from the gallery, but in a move of dubious constitutionality, he appointed members of the cabinet as acting ministers and argued that they did not have to resign. The tactic gave an angry, bitter King his opportunity: if the acting ministers had taken the oath of office, he argued, they had to resign; if they had not taken the oath they had no business running their departments. It seemed a sensible argument, and convinced many of the Progressives who had never wanted to see a high-tariff Meighen government in office. When the votes were counted, Meighen had lost by one vote, and that vote was cast by a Progressive who claimed he was so excited he forgot he was paired with an absent Conservative and should not have voted. But the government had been defeated. Meighen immediately secured a dissolution.

The 1926 election gave King a solid majority. A year later, Meighen was replaced as Conservative leader by R.B. Bennett, who, when he became prime minister, sent Meighen to the Senate, where he became government leader. In 1941, as the King government sought to avoid conscription during the Second War, the Tories again turned to Meighen, whose views on that matter had not changed at all. Meighen accepted the leadership, and contested a by-election in Toronto. Terrified by the prospect of Meighen returning to the Commons, King wisely did not run a Liberal candidate and encouraged the party machine and voters to throw their support behind the unknown c.c.f. candidate. The tactic worked. Meighen retired from politics, but continued to work and to justify his actions in 1926 until he died in 1960. He titled a book of his speeches: Unrevised and Unrepented. He had been, and still is, a controversial figure, but as Eugene Forsey has so aptly expressed it, Meighen had "strode up the great bare staircase of his duty, as he saw it, uncheered and undismayed."

The Painting:

King was like beach grass holding the land together; it bends with the wind. Meighen was like a strong and imposing house, rigid and unable to bounce back. In a hurricane, the strength of the house is its weakness. It is too rigid to withstand force, while beach grass bends and survives. It was the roaring, sexy twenties but Meighen was a Victorian sensibility, rigid and unyielding. I have a high opinion of Meighen, but a Prime Minister must have more than intelligence. He was the most difficult to paint and the last completed. I always had vertical stripes in mind. Their upward thrust, though static, is strong and positive. The twin arrows emphasize this thrust. There is repose in the softer horizontal strokes. Areas seem hidden and remote, at a distance, as Meighen was from the public. Because of his personality and style I feel Meighen would fare better today with tv, etc. The painting has an ethereal feeling. It is the third highest in the series, emphasizing the positive upward thrust. In terms of pure, native intelligence, he was the only PM who measured up to Trudeau. But, out of sync with his times, he could not apply his intellectual ability to the wider requirements of his role. He did not have the pragmatic flexibility of Trudeau. Still, I felt myself strongly drawn to him.

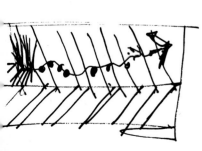

MANY HAVE taken it as a personal insult, certainly a sad reflection on their country, that William Lyon Mackenzie King could have been leader of the Liberal party for almost thirty years and Prime Minister for over twenty. His opponents were mystified and outraged, and many supporters, if they did not despise him, extended only grudging respect. His political life was a shell game, with policy the pea. Though not the most hated, Mackenzie King was probably the least loved of all Canadian Prime Ministers.

He was the strangest of men, far stranger than his contemporaries knew. He was shy, terribly lonely, insecure, friendless, with an insatiable desire to be liked but a pitiful awareness that he was not. His best friend was his Irish terrier, Pat, who was always an attentive listener and King taught him to play the piano. With no friends in this world, except his neighbour, Joan Patteson, with whom he spent long but never clandestine hours, he communicated with them in the other world through mediums, table-rapping sessions, and, above all his dreams, dutifully recorded and interpreted to his satisfaction in his diary. The diary is a gold mine for psychiatrists, as King wrestled with his love for his mother, his ambivalence towards his father, his physical attraction to women but his dread of carnal love or knowledge. He seemed attracted to prostitutes, to women in scarlet, some say for their sexual favours, others to make them see the evil of their ways. It was a somewhat sordid, comic night life for a prim power-broker. Coincidences – the hands on the clock, a chance meeting, a familiar tune – were constantly reassuring, a sign of some divine presence telling him that he was not alone. King might have enjoyed life, but he took it too seriously, and a late evening of dancing left him full of remorse, scolding himself: "My position, work & self-respect all demand less in the way of dancing."

In his day and ours, people marvel at the success of the pudgy rotund little man who seemed to have none of the qualities of a successful political leader. He lacked Macdonald's conviviality, Laurier's ease; he had no platform presence, no charisma in public or private; his speeches were long and tedious, pretentious and platitudinous, leaving the impression with one journalist that he was "floundering about like a man on a sandbar who is not sure how far the tide is going to rise." But King was intensely ambitious. He was perhaps the most politically astute leader in the nation's history, sensitive to every nuance, alert to every danger, and he had courage, the kind of courage it takes to sit on a powder keg never certain when it might blow up.

He was born in Kitchener on December 17, 1874, the son of John King and Isabel Mackenzie, the daughter of the rebel of 1837, and it is as Mackenzie King that we know him. His father was weak, his mother a woman with a powerful personality, determined that her son would make up for the wrongs history had done to a man who had fought for self-government, for wresting power from privileged classes. King lived under his mother's shadow until he died, and from the after-life above she watched over his every act. King studied law at Toronto, where he crossed paths with Arthur Meighen, but his interests led him to economics and sociology, and to an interest in the social problems of an industrial society. Graduate work at Chicago and Harvard was followed by an invitation to move to Ottawa and organize the Department of Labour. In 1908, he was elected to the House of Commons, and a year later he entered Laurier's cabinet as the first Minister of Labour. Defeated in 1911 and again in 1917, when he ran as a Laurier Liberal, he worked as a labour conciliator for the Rockefellers and other large corporations in the United States and wrote a book called, Industry and Humanity.

But all the while he maintained his contacts with the Liberal party, preparing for the day when he would contest the leadership. The day came in 1919, when Laurier died. The favourite seemed to be the Nova Scotian, W.S. Fielding, a close colleague of Laurier's since 1896, but Fielding had supported conscription and King had not. With the backing of almost the entire Québec contingent, Mackenzie King was elected on the third ballot. "It is right, it is the call of duty,"

49

King wrote sanctimoniously in his diary. "I have sought nothing, it has come. It has come from God." For the next two years, King worked hard to reunite the Liberal party. The onset of a post-war recession in 1920 came to his aid, and in the election of 1921 he won a narrow victory as Québec gave him every seat and the Progressives swept much of Ontario and all of the west. For the next four years, King wooed the Progressives, throwing modest tariff decreases their way, and also consolidating his position in Québec. But voters were not impressed with what seemed like a lack-lustre government, so while he gained seats in the prairies and maintained his hold on Québec, Ontario and the Maritimes went decisively against him in the 1925 election.

It looked like King's career was over, for he had not shored up his position as leader firmly enough to withstand possible challenges to his leadership. But King grimly hung on to power, much to Governor General Lord Byng's displeasure and Meighen's outrage, hoping that if he could survive for a session in Parliament he could then secure another dissolution and, with the return of better times, secure a majority. But the customs scandal, which removed Progressive support, and Lord Byng's determination, forced King to contest the 1926 election as leader of the opposition, not Prime Minister. King tried to make Byng's action the issue in the election, and for the rest of his life was persuaded that he had, but it was really the final disintegration of the Progressives and large gains in Ontario and the west that brought King back to power: Meighen had been hoist on the tariff petard and King had survived, his hold on the party secure. During the boom years of the late twenties, King was able to lower tariffs, balance the budget, reduce taxes, and vastly improve the management of that albatross he had inherited from the Borden government, the Canadian National Railways. But the stock market crash and the collapse of the world economy in 1929 brought the good times to a sudden end. As prices fell, farmers demanded more protection; as factories closed down, unemployment passed ten and then thirteen percent. King had no answers, indeed he denied that the country faced a serious problem. R.B. Bennett, the new Conservative leader, claimed that he did, and the voters were more than prepared to give him a chance, even in Québec. King spent five long years in opposition, as Bennett watched the depression and western drought sink the country to its knees. King kept his party united as the Tories fell apart and the CCF and Social Credit sprung forth to offer their road to economic salvation. KING OR CHAOS – that, said the Liberals, was the choice in 1935 – and although King really had little to offer, Bennett was so thoroughly discredited and the newer parties had such a limited appeal, that King was back in power. He remained there until he retired thirteen years later. In most parts of the country, the worst of the depression was over by 1935, although it was only with the coming of the Second War that the Canadian economy returned to anything like full employment. King's government passed some useful legislation, and he appointed a royal commission which was to recommend radical changes in the structure of the Canadian federal system. But increasingly, King's attention was focussed on the coming storm in Europe.

The key to King's success lay in his sense of what the Canadian community was, his view of the role of government, and his style or philosophy of political leadership. King understood and accepted the highly pluralistic nature of Canadian society: a country of provinces and regions, of widely differing economic interests, of races – above all French and English – religions, and social and political attitudes. "In a country like ours," he wrote, "it is particularly true that the art of government is largely one of seeking to reconcile rather than to exaggerate differences – to come as near to the happy mean." Government did not exist to weld Canada into one, to force a single policy on the entire country, to be the agent of dramatic social change. Government should march in step with public opinion, remedying abuses, aiding the unfortunate, preventing exploitation. "The meek were to be protected," wrote his biographer Blair Neatby, "but it was not the function of government to arrange for them to inherit the earth."

And the instrument for the grand work of conciliation was the Liberal Party. The party itself should be a microcosm of the nation – of the liberally-minded section of the nation – which really excluded only unrepentant Imperialists and protectionists, and those on the far left who wished to see a planned and regimented society. The parliamentary caucus and the cabinet were King's sounding board. He was not an authoritarian leader. He listened to caucus, he consulted caucus, he believed that all policies should find a consensus in caucus. The same was true of his cabinet. King selected strong and able lieutenants from all parts of the country. Once again, he sought concensus and, as he once said, "Such success as I had had with government and with my Parliament was the result of allowing my colleagues their fair share of responsibility of consideration of policy." King, of course, often tried to form that concensus, to give direction, to persuade and sometimes cajole, but very rarely did he demand that his way be followed. If labels there must be, Mackenzie King was the Great Conciliator. And it was his view that if the Liberal Party could be kept united, so could the country. An added benefit was that he and the party were likely to remain in power, and his critics could argue that the obsession with national unity, the everlasting search for concensus through compromise, was simply a crude political calculus. And to others, like the left-wing poet Frank Scott –

> He blunted us.
> We had no shape
> Because he never took sides,
> And no sides
> Because he never allowed them to take shape.

King's woolly rhetoric and deliberately clouded ambiguities, his refusal to take a strong and firm position, did seem almost immoral to intellectuals like Scott and someone like Meighen whose slogan, like Luther's, might have been: Here I Stand. But it created a united party and, as Canada moved towards the Second World War, a more or less united country.

That Canada declared war in 1939 a more or less united country owed as much to Mackenzie King as to Hitler. As late as June 1938, the British High Commissioner in Ottawa informed his London superiors that Canada could not be relied upon if Britain went to war, for Mackenzie King was concerned above all with "what he considers to be the main objective, viz. the preservation of Canada's unity," and was determined "again and again to insist on the supremacy of Parliament as the interpreter of the people's wishes if and when the time comes. He refuses resolutely to take any other line."

Since 1921, Mackenzie King had followed the same line. He was a nationalist and an isolationist, and the two were mutually reinforcing. As a Canadian nationalist, he was determined to secure the independence and equality of Canada without cutting the tie with Britain. As an isolationist, he was determined to free Canada from any automatic commitments to go to war on behalf of either Britain or the League of Nations, for he knew how a European war could rupture the tender fabric of Canadian unity. King's "parliament will decide" response to a British request for military assistance in 1922 was in striking contrast to Meighen's "Ready Aye Ready." A year later, at the Imperial Conference he refused to accept the British view that there should be a common Imperial foreign policy, and insisted that Canadian policy would be made by and for Canadians. And at the Imperial Conference of 1926, King helped draft the famous statement describing the Dominions as "autonomous communities within the British Empire, equal in status, in no way subordinate one to another in any aspect of their domestic or external affairs, though united by a common allegiance to the Crown and freely associated as members of the British Commonwealth of Nations."

King followed the same policy of freedom of action and no commitments as a member of the League of Nations. He refused to underwrite the borders of Europe, repudiated the Canadian delegate in 1935 when he proposed the imposition of oil sanctions in an effort to halt Mussolini's invasion of Ethiopia, and as Hitler openly defied the League, urged that "emphasis should be placed upon conciliation rather than coercion." He made it clear that Canada was not prepared to accept "automatic commitments to the application of force." For the next three years, King endorsed the policy of appeasement, refusing any obligation other than – parliament will decide when pressed to declare firmly for neutrality or to state that

Canada would be at Britain's side. By 1939, King realized war was inevitable, and he knew also that when it came Canada would be in it. But he had made no commitments, he had done everything possible to avoid it, and the decision would be made in Canada. He trusted that when war came Canadians would realize that a war against Hitler, beside Britain and France, was their war, too. He was right, and the result of his inglorious foreign policy was that an almost united country independently declared war in September, 1939.

King was immediately challenged by Maurice Duplessis, the Union Nationale premier of Québec, who charged that the assumption of vast wartime powers by Ottawa would destroy the autonomy of Québec, and that once again the war would lead to conscription. The challenge could not be ignored. Already King and his alter ego from Québec, Ernest Lapointe, had promised there would be no conscription for overseas service, and Lapointe entered the campaign to repeat his pledge and announce his determination to resign if Duplessis won: an action which would lead to a Tory or coalition government that would make conscription inevitable. The strategy worked, and Duplessis was defeated. The next challenge came from Ontario, where Mitchell Hepburn, King's inveterate enemy, passed a resolution at Queen's Park denouncing the government for doing too little. King seized the opportunity and called an immediate federal election, and swamped the Tories.

King had hoped that Canada's contribution would be in munitions and supplies, her military commitment largely in the air. The economic contribution was enormous, and after the fall of western Europe and before the Japanese accelerated America's entry into the war in December 1941, Canada was second only to Britain in defence of the west. But the war demanded military contributions, too. The first division was overseas in December 1939, and pilots of the RCAF were in the air during the battle of Britain. At the peak in 1944, there were over three quarter of a million men and women in uniform, half of them overseas.

But from the outset of the war, conscription was an issue. Many Canadians, members of King's cabinet among them, were conscriptionists on principle. After the fall of France, King responded to pressure and to the need for more men by introducing compulsory service, but only for service in Canada. By 1942, anticipating future needs and pressed from all sides, King was forced to ask the Canadian people in a plebiscite to release his government from the promise not to use conscription for overseas service. It was, he said, "Not necessarily conscription, but conscription if necessary." English Canada voted over 80 percent Yes, while Québec voted over 70 percent No. French Canada was almost unanimous, and, with some logic and justice, argued that it was English Canada that had voted to release the government from a pledge it had made to Québec. By 1944, heavy infantry casualties in Europe far outdistanced recruiting, and the demands to send the so-called "zombies" who refused to volunteer for active service became overwhelming. But King was determined to avoid conscription, the rupture of 1917 never far from his mind. He dismissed his conscriptionist Defence Minister, Colonel Ralston, in the hope that General McNaughton could persuade men to volunteer. But the general failed, and King had no choice. Louis St. Laurent, who had replaced Lapointe as King's Québec lieutenant, agreed. In the House of Commons, King made perhaps the greatest speech of his life: "If there is anything to which I have devoted my political life, it is to try to promote unity, harmony and amity between the diverse elements of this country. My friends can desert me, they can remove their confidence from me, they can withdraw the trust they have placed in my hands, but never shall I deviate from that line of policy. Whatever may be the consequences, whether loss of prestige, loss of popularity, or loss of power, I feel that I am right, and I know that a time will come when every man will render me full justice on that score." The time has come, and today most people would agree that bringing Canada through the War without the deep and lasting scars that followed the First War was King's greatest accomplishment. Of course, there was enormous opposition in Québec, but even in the Commons, nineteen French Canadian members supported him. In the end, less than 2500 conscripts were sent to the front. Sixty-nine were killed.

All the while, King's government had been planning for the

post-war world. A new generation of scholars and bureaucrats, brought up on Lord Keynes and the new economics, developed post-war policies that foresaw a very active and interventionist role for the central government. The government, they argued, had to be responsible for maintaining a high level of employment and income, and through family allowances, improved pensions, medical and hospital care and other social programs, make certain that the new post-war world would be far better than the old. This new Canada was years in the making, but the recipe was on the table before Mackenzie King retired on November 14, 1948. He died amidst his collected ruins at Kingsmere on July 22, 1950. He was buried under a simple plaque in Toronto's Mount Pleasant cemetery.

The Painting:

As a child, it seemed that Mackenzie King had been Prime Minister forever. I recall images of him in sepia tones creeping through the rotogravure sections of the Toronto Star Weekly. A strange fellow who walked around the garden a lot. I would have liked to listen in on his conversations with his mother. Back in those days, I hardly knew who Foster Hewitt was, but King was a real presence. He seemed controversial, dominant, and unloved.

He used to be seen as dull and gray, withdrawn into himself. This spiritual man must also have been a spirited man. His political brilliance and skill at manoeuvre show a concern with larger conceptions and a real zest for challenge. For a long time, those rotogravure sepia tones represented King, but I found that underneath there was a personality with real depth and a quiet vibrancy. King will never be easy to grasp. There are so many aspects to the man that I could do ten paintings of him. The actual work is suggestive, symbolic and expressionistic, and the palette, which is unusual for me, bears some relationship to camouflage, his secret life, I suppose. It has a slightly veiled, eerie quality, unintentional but there: his eerieness lies in the difference one finds between a

white witch and a black witch: there was no profound evil in the man. The skull is generalized to King, his spiritualism, but also the grave issues he had to face. There is a stiffness in the vertical stripes, forming a barrier. King, in a sense, was a prisoner of himself and his role.

Women were an important, difficult part of his life. The two-headed dog is a duality. It seemed to me there were many dualities in King: his public and private lives; his desire to reform, the practicalities of keeping political power; Britain and the United States; the English and French in Canada. The words 'King-Byng Wing Ding' appear across the triptych. This dramatic manoeuvre summed up King's desire for power, his sense of Canadian independence, and his political skill. What came out of that was of great importance to the country and the Commonwealth. I have done a small painting called King-Byng Wing Ding.

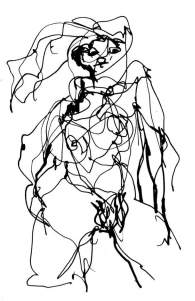

Working study: oil 20" × 20"
KING-BYNG WING DING

57

The rendering of the painting is loose, considering its scale. I wanted to present diversity within a whole. It bears some similarity to doodles, the unconscious coming through. The painting has an edge, not a border, and the images float. I was going to carry the painting further, but when the sun hit it I stood back and realized that if I went further I would be super-imposing another painting. When I finished, I had a feeling King would like it, secretly. I could see it candle-lit in Laurier House with King sitting in front of it in a captain's chair, his dog by his side.

I T'S IRONIC that in the worst of times, the great depression, one of Canada's richest men was Prime Minister. Bennett is scarcely remembered now, but he was a household word: there were Bennett Buggies (horse-pulled cars whose owners could afford neither gas nor repairs); Eggs Bennett (boiled chestnuts); Bennett blankets (yesterday's newspaper); and Bennetburghs (the villages of tar-paper shacks which sheltered the unemployed and homeless). "One of the greatest assets a man can have on entering life's struggle," he told a group of students who faced a bleak future, "is poverty."

There was, however, no silver spoon in his mouth when Bennett was born. His father's shipping business had failed not long after he was born in Hopewell, New Brunswick, in 1870, and the old man, easy-going and inclined to drink, couldn't restore the family fortunes. Every cent had to count in the Bennett household, and after getting a teacher's certificate, Bennett taught to earn money to go to Dalhousie law school. Practicing for a few years in Chatham, Bennett moved to Calgary where he soon built up a solid reputation and a flourishing practice as a corporation lawyer associated with Senator James Lougheed, the grandfather of a later premier of Alberta. Profitable investments in Turner Valley oil and in some of the giant corporate mergers, executed by his friend Max Aitken, later Lord Beaverbrook, soon made him a wealthy man, and by 1914 his investment income alone amounted to over $30,000 a year, and by 1919 it had doubled. Two years later, his old Chatham friend, Jennie Sheriff, who had married a much older E.B. Eddy, inheriting much of his wealth, died and left him almost half a million dollars in Eddy shares. The death of her brother in 1926, left him $5,000,000 more and control of the company. When Bennett became prime minister in 1930, he was a multi-millionaire with an annual income of $300,000. He was unquestionably the richest Prime Minister in Canadian history.

Bennett had been interested in politics since his days in Chatham, and as a staunch believer in the Empire he was a committed Conservative. Elected first to the Alberta legislature, he switched to federal politics in 1911 and sat in the Commons until 1917. Defeated in the 1921 election, he was successful in 1925 and remained as the member for Calgary until he retired from politics in 1938. Although many were concerned about Bennett's imperious manner, he was the choice of the party establishment to succeed Meighen as Tory leader in 1927 and won handily in a spotty field on the second ballot.

For the next three years Bennett gave tirelessly of his energy and his wealth to build up the Conservative Party and his own image as a strong and decisive leader. Fortune came to his aid in 1930 as the country slid into a depression. King seemed to have no answer; indeed, he denied that anything like a depression existed. As conditions worsened, Bennett thundered that he and he alone had an answer to the depression: "Mackenzie King promises you conferences. I promise you action. He promises consideration of unemployment. I promise to end unemployment."

As farmers faced falling prices and the ranks of the unemployed grew, Bennett pointed across the border: "They have the jobs and we have the soup kitchens." The Liberals championed free trade, but, "Tell me, when did free trade fight for you. You say our tariffs are only for the manufacturers: I will make them fight for you as well. I will use them to blast a way into the markets that have been closed to you." It was heady stuff, delivered with all the bombast and certainty of a Methodist preacher at a revival meeting – for a fervent Methodist Bennett was – and it was convincing to an electorate promised nothing by Mackenzie King. And in 1930, R.B. Bennett became Prime Minister of Canada.

The new Prime Minister had an intense sense of mission, an ambition so strong that he could not accept the thought of failure and had a total incapacity to work with others. His one biographer has concluded that it was all his mother's fault, a mother who was determined to make of her sons, particularly Richard, the man her husband never was. The son became the receptacle of his mother's love, her ambitions, her frustrations. In short, Bennett was a neurotic. "That alone can explain his furious energy, his driving ambition, his resentment of competition, his moods of despair, his inability to work with others on terms of equality, his outbursts of temper, his apparent arrogance and insensitivity to those around him." (His brother George was neurotic, too, but he simply quietly drank himself to death while Bennett remained a teetotaler all his life). Bennett certainly adored his mother, but whatever the explanation, the description of Bennett's character was endorsed by his contemporaries. As one of his colleagues bitterly remarked: "He is disgustingly conceited and feels he outweighs all other Canadians in importance. He is contemptuous of the intelligence and efforts of others – in every respect a lone wolf (except perhaps in the rutting season when, of course, no other males are welcome)." Bennett, who lived in suites in the Palliser Hotel and the Château Laurier, was attracted to women, but never married.

For five years, he ran almost a one-man government, a government of the first person singular. A story went the rounds of Ottawa that a tourist saw a familiar face walking up the hill to the Parliament buildings and asked a native who he was. "That's the Prime Minister," was the reply. "Why is he talking to himself?" asked the tourist. "Oh, he's having a cabinet meeting."

Six weeks after the election, Bennett had a special session of Parliament to approve a grant of $20,000,000 – to assist the hard-pressed provinces and municipalities help the unemployed, largely through public works projects, and to raise the tariff to astronomical heights. But the depression deepened, the situation made even more critical by devastating drought on the prairies. By 1933, close to thirty percent of the workers were unemployed, and a million-and-a-half people were dependent on government relief for food and shelter. Desperate men were attracted to new ideologies, and the Communist Party, masquerading as the Workers' Unity League, found fertile ground, particularly among single men. There were tens of thousands of them, riding the rods from east to west, west to east, hounded by the police as they gathered along the railroad tracks or panhandled on the streets of Vancouver and Calgary, Winnipeg and Toronto. Bennett's answer was work camps run by the military, where single men could work far from the cities for twenty cents a day and food that ranged from bad to indifferent. There was no life outside the camp, no entertainment, no women, and no booze.

Open dissent was met with force. Across Canada, May Day demonstrations were broken up as city police charged marchers and arrested speakers. The RCMP infiltrated the Communist Party and Bennett, who equated socialism with Communism, promised to crush the Reds under "the iron heel of ruthlessness." Tim Buck and other leaders of the Communist Party were arrested and thrown into the penitentiary at Kingston. A delegation of workers coming to present their case to him on Parliament Hill faced an armoured car and armed detachments of the RCMP. And on July 1, 1935, the RCMP and city police broke up a meeting of ON TO OTTAWA trekkers in Regina, leaving one detective killed and scores of trekkers injured.

Long before then, however, Bennett had realized that the depression would not yield to his rhetoric, that relief was a palliative not a cure, and that the tariff was of little value to Canadian producers. In 1933 and 1934, he tried to find new markets, created the Bank of Canada to regulate the flow of credit and currency and stimulate the economy, provided additional credit to farmers, initiated a study of unemployment insurance, and allowed H.H. Stevens, one of his cabinet ministers, to begin an investigation of the buying practices of large companies like Eaton's and Simpson's, which seemed to lead to a remarkable spread between the prices paid to producers and the cost to the consumer.

Despite these signs of a new mood in Ottawa, the country was astonished when Bennett took to the air in January 1935 to announce his New Deal. His speeches were influenced and partly written by his brother-in-law, William Herridge, ambassador to Washington who had been impressed by the boldness and political impact, if not the content, of Roosevelt's New Deal. But not even FDR went as far in attacking the old order as R.B. Bennett, the millionaire autocrat. "The old order is gone," he thundered in his first speech. "It will not return.... I am for reform. And, in my mind, reform means Government intervention. It means Government control and regulation. It means the end of laissez faire." – My God, the Prime Minister has gone mad," exclaimed a Montreal newspaper when, in his third speech, Bennett launched an attack on his onetime friends, the capitalists, who it now seemed had corrupted the profit system:

"Selfish men, and this country is not without them – men whose mounting bankrolls loom larger than your happiness, corporations without souls and without virtue – these, fearful that this Government might impinge on what they have grown to regard as their immemorial right of exploitation, will whisper against us. They will call us radicals. They will say that this is the first step on the road to socialism. We fear them not."

And finally, in his last speech, a call to arms: "The issue is clearly defined. If you are satisfied with conditions as they are, support Liberalism. If you want no changes in the capitalist system, declare for that party.... for Liberalism stands for laissez faire and the unrestricted operation of the profit system and the complete freedom of capitalism to do as it thinks right or to do as it thinks wrong."

The legislation Bennett brought to Parliament that spring was less frightening: minimum wages and the eight hour day, assistance to farmers and other producers through government control of marketing and prices, unemployment insurance, and stricter controls over company financing to protect the investor. King refused to oppose the legislation, content to argue that most of it was an invasion of provincial authority and therefore unconstitutional.

Bennett faced the people in the fall of 1935 with his New Deal broadcasts still ringing in their ears. But the voters were not convinced by what the CCF leader, J.S. Woodsworth, called a "deathbed conversion." Over a million cast their ballots for the CFF, for Social Credit, and for Steven's Reconstruction Party – a party championing the rights of small business, producers and consumers against the power of the big corporations. Bennett's support fell below thirty percent of the electorate, and Mackenzie King, appearing under banners proclaiming it was KING OR CHAOS – uttering platitudes such as, "What is needed more than a change of economic structure is a change of heart," got back his office in the East Block.

Bennett left behind him a shattered party, one that did not recover for over twenty years. In 1938, he resigned as leader and retired to

London, where his old friend Lord Beaverbrook got him a title and a seat in the House of Lords as Viscount Bennett of Mickleham, Calgary and Hopewell – a title little more distinguished than the irreverent Mitch Hepburn's, Lord Gopher of Calgary. Occasionally, he went to the House of Lords, often he was busy supporting a variety of philanthropic activities and institutions in Canada, including a gift of $750,000 to the Dalhousie Law School. He died a lonely old man, boiled to death in a bath tub in England on June 26, 1947, the public still unsure about his New Deal, whether it was the political opportunism his opponents said it was, or a conversion to the necessities of an interventionist state.

The Painting:

I painted the "Bennett times" more than the man. He was a tycoon, a right-wing character who found himself sponsoring government intervention. In the end, he was rich and lonely. His loneliness did not touch me as deeply as the terrible times.

When I was a boy, I worked for my father, a market gardener. We lived in a house rented for seventeen dollars a month, heated by a coal and wood stove. This was only seventy miles from Toronto. We would sometimes eat porridge and have bread and milk for dessert, and my mother made mittens for me out of men's socks. We were lucky because my father grew food and we weren't considered poor. I remember the hobos coming to the door for food and relatives reduced to nothing. It was a time of anguish. Every person who went through it, especially the creative, carry its mark. It's not the mark of Cain, it's the mark of Abel.

The canvas has a nightmarish, surreal quality about it. There is a horizon line, but the blue above is not pleasant. It has darkness about it. The area below, which might be the earth in a landscape painting, is not the colour of Canada. It is Naples yellow. The Naples yellow represents the prairies and the drought that hit that part of the country. The large black shape could be many things, but it surely shows the anguish and violence of that terrible period. The bottom is raw and unfinished. This is a passionate painting carrying with it a sense of cold foreboding. There is despair in the black but the crimson shows hope. I painted the times and perhaps didn't do Bennett justice. He did try to respond to the chaos by seeking new directions, launching initiatives.

Louis St. Laurent was the least political of all Canada's Prime Ministers. A brilliant corporation lawyer, he was sixty when he entered politics, moving with avuncular style from corporate to cabinet board rooms. While Mackenzie King never made a decision without long and anxious consideration of the political ramifications, St. Laurent, as one cabinet colleague said, "with his sharp lawyer's mind made a decision by removing the human element from it and working it out like an algebraic equation. Then he tried to make it fit political reality." It was his strength and his weakness.

St. Laurent entered King's cabinet out of duty, in December 1941, just three days after Pearl Harbour, when the death of Ernest Lapointe left King without a Québec lieutenant – and Québec without political leadership. His job was to help maintain national unity as the government worked its way through the tortuous conscription issue, and he agreed only to serve for the duration.

St. Laurent was superbly equipped for the job. The son of a shopkeeper in Compton, Québec, where he was born in 1882, the young boy grew up in a bilingual home, speaking French to his father and English to his Irish-Canadian mother. It was only when he went to school that he realized not everyone was bilingual. Raised as a strict Roman Catholic, he lived next to a Methodist Church and he once said that the only difference he saw between Protestant and Catholic was that the poor Protestant children were not allowed out to play on Sundays. While he remained above all else a French Canadian, referring often to "my people, my race," he was also a firm believer in the Canadian partnership, and even graced it with some divine purpose. "You know the men at the head of government are only instruments to carry out the plans of Providence," and "I am convinced that Wolfe and Montcalm were merely the instruments of an all-powerful Providence to create a situation where the descendants of the two great races would find themselves together on this northern part of the American continent." Like Trudeau after him, he believed that French Canadians should not closet themselves in Québec, but should play their role in the government of the country. And when pressed to take the prime ministership in 1948, he accepted to prove that Laurier would not stand alone as the only French Canadian Catholic to preside over the destiny of the Canadian partnership.

Uncle Louie, the grand patriarch of the Canadian family, guided the nation through the difficult but prosperous decade after the Second War. He did not run a one-man government, and the government was not prisoner to the past. Post-war policies were devised by a young and talented group of civil servants, men of the twentieth not the nineteenth century, who saw a new role for Canada in the world, and, for the federal government a new role in federation. His cabinet ministers – Pearson, Martin, Howe – were given the freedom to run their own departments. The cabinet acted like a board of directors, with St. Laurent the amiable, but cooly efficient, chairman of the board. He gave Canada sound and efficient government, and was re-elected in 1949 and 1953, but in the end the Liberals became insensitive to the changing mood in Canada and reaped the inevitable reward in 1957.

As Secretary of State for External Affairs for two years after the War, and later as Prime Minister – with Mike Pearson in External Affairs – Louis St. Laurent launched Canada boldly into a new role as a middle power. He was one of the first to see the dangers for Canada in the cold peace, and helped in the creation of NATO, entered the Korean War without hesitation, sent Canadian troops to Europe – all a far cry from the policy of no commitments. During the famous Suez crisis in 1956, when Britain, France and Israel attacked Egypt, he openly opposed their actions and worked tirelessly to keep NATO, the Commonwealth and the American alliance together as Pearson sought to improvise a UN peacekeeping force that could defuse the crisis – winning for himself the Nobel Prize. Britain, led by the doddering if not dotty Anthony Eden, had counted on Canadian support, and there were those in Canada, particularly in the Conservative Party, who cried again that Canada's response should have been: Ready Aye Ready, and drove St. Laurent to exclaim that, "The era when the supermen of Europe could govern the whole world is coming pretty close to an end."

At home, St. Laurent perceived a new role for the federal government. He had chaired the committee preparing for post-war reconstruction, and was convinced that the federal government should not be the passive bystander it was under King, but should take the lead in attacking the problems of unemployment, inequalities among the regions and provinces, and provide adequate pensions for the old and health care for the poor in cooperation with the provinces. It was under his administration that the foundations for the Canadian welfare state were laid, and a new era in federal-provincial cooperation – or conflict – was begun.

St. Laurent was also a Canadian nationalist. Newfoundland entered Confederation. Appeals to the Judicial Committee were abolished. In 1952, he appointed Vincent Massey as the first Canadian Governor General. Earlier, he had appointed Massey as chairman of a royal commission to examine Canadian culture, then a puny infant overwhelmed by its American cousin, and on its recommendations gave financial aid to Canadian universities and later, despite St. Laurent's dislike for "subsidizing ballet dancing," created the Canada Council.

Canada boomed during the St. Laurent years: construction of the massive St. Lawrence Seaway and the Trans-Canada Highway, exploitation of the rich oil and gas resources of the west, discovery of new fields of minerals and iron ore, and bountiful prairie harvests bringing new wealth to the country. The economic boom brought hundreds of thousands of immigrants from Britain and war-torn Europe, many of them refugees from expansion of the Soviet empire, such as the 35,000 Hungarians who fled the 1956 invasion.

But much of the new investment was American. The new factories that sprung up across the country were often American branch plants, and Canadian trade was increasingly tied to American markets. By the middle 50s, there was fear that culturally and economically Canada was becoming an American satellite, independent only in name. These fears surfaced in 1956, when C.D. Howe – St. Laurent's "minister of everything" to do with economic development – became convinced that Canada needed a pipeline to carry Alberta's natural gas to central Canadian markets. The pipeline was to be built by a corporation largely American-controlled, and one that needed government assistance if it was to be started and finished on schedule. When Howe attempted to ram a bill providing the aid through Parliament, resorting finally to the use of closure in the face of an opposition filibuster, the Conservatives had an interlocking network of issues that won the 1957 election: the St. Laurent Liberals were portrayed as anti-British, pro-American, insensitive to public opinion, arrogant in the use of power, and contemptuous of the rights of Parliament. That the government only raised old age pensions six dollars a month at a time of apparent prosperity was another indication that there were too few politicians in the Liberal board room.

Soon after his defeat by John Diefenbaker in 1957, Louis St. Laurent resigned the Liberal leadership, and Lester Pearson, the hero of Suez, succeeded him. St. Laurent retired to his study and the warmth of the family he had so much missed during his sixteen years in politics. He died in Québec City on July 25, 1973.

The Painting:

Louis St. Laurent was the right man at the right time. His times were good for the country. If he'd been born earlier, in the dust times of the depression, he might have been a disaster. A photograph of Louis St. Laurent stuck in my mind, a black and white image. He looked out with dark, deeply-set eyes, pleasant but not smiling, wearing a dark, expensive overcoat, a glimpse of pin-stripe suit, a white silk scarf, and a Homburg. He looked substantial, avuncular. The painting is serene with a defined border which contains a solid central image: dominant but not overbearing. It is my sense of the enclosed ritual of Catholicism, and also recalls the fact that some party pro said that if St. Laurent died they'd stuff him anyway and run him again. It has a formality and strength, the character of an icon, perhaps a corporate icon, blue and white, colours which are, for me, not only the colours of Québec, but Canada. In the central image, the white lines are a little like pin stripes, or all that remains of a silk scarf and dark coat. His prestige and elegance are there, a studied serenity representative of the man.

I N 1958, one long finger wagged in the country's eye. John Diefenbaker, the prairie populist, was a presence with his accusative tone, his piercing, often fierce eyes, the tight curly hair making a V on his forehead, the flow of unfinished sentences promising fire in the boondocks of hell to his enemies and earthly paradise to friends. All his adult life John Diefenbaker wanted to be Prime Minister. He won the greatest electoral victory in Canadian history. Within a decade he was defeated, discredited, cast aside, a tragic figure.

He was born in 1895 in Neustadt, Ontario, not far from Owen Sound. He liked to pose as the first Prime Minister of neither French nor English origin, and in a strict sense, it was true. But the Diefenbakers had been in Canada since 1816, and on his mother's side, he descended from Scots Highlanders. His father, a teacher, moved to Saskatchewan to homestead at the turn of the century, teaching on the side and finally taking a government job in Saskatoon. The son was a hard worker, physically strong, an avid reader, and – so the family has it – looked up from a book on Laurier to announce: "I'm going to be Premier of Canada, some day." In later years, Diefenbaker used to tell his corn-ball story of how, in 1910, he sold a newspaper to Laurier at the Saskatoon railroad platform and after a brief conversation told the Prime Minister he was too busy to talk and had to get back to selling papers.

His mother (and maternal power is one thread that binds many, many of our Prime Ministers together) had an enormous influence on him and it was she who vetoed his plan to enter a bank and sent him instead to University, where he edited the student newspaper and starred on the debating team. After graduating in 1916, he joined the Canadian army, but was invalided home soon after his arrival in Britain. He returned to university to take a law degree, and was a success as a lawyer, developing a rhetorical court room skill. He seemed to flourish with unpopular cases, and won 18 of the 20 murder cases he undertook.

But his ambition lay in politics. Less determined men would have given up after five defeats – federally and provincially, and even an attempt to become mayor of Prince Albert. But Diefenbaker persevered, and was finally elected to the House of Commons in 1940. He soon made an impression in the House as a skilled partisan debater, a prairie populist much different from the pin-striped Tories from the east. "Why, Diefenbaker's so far ahead of some of the members of our Party," exclaimed a farmer friend, that when he went down there, he was sometimes referred to as "the Bolshevik from the west." But the western Bolshevik ran a poor third at the 1942 leadership convention. Six years later, he tried again, pitting himself against George Drew, the Bay Street favourite. "I will not, if chosen leader, offer something for nothing," he promised the convention. "I will require of you, my fellow Canadians, all the energy, all the faith and all the vision that the Canadians of yesterday gave to the foundation of the nation." He was trounced on the first ballot, and thereafter distrusted the eastern establishment, a distrust that was more than reciprocated. But in 1956, he tried again, and although the same old guard went all out to defeat him, the convention decided that it was time, as his nominator said, for "a man who always comes to the aid of the misunderstood, the forgotten, the underprivileged, and those suffering from what he considers to be an injustice." He won on the first ballot.

Diefenbaker did not win the 1957 election. The Liberals lost it. But his stinging attacks on their arrogance, their insensitivity, their abuse of parliament, their parsimony, their refusal to adopt policies of national development that would arrest the drift to continentalism, certainly helped. Once in office at the head of a minority government – he had 112 seats to the Liberals 105 and the minor parties 48 – he lowered taxes, increased pensions, and when the Liberals foolishly suggested he turn power back to them, he turned it back to the people instead.

The 1958 election is the one remembered. "Without a Vision the people perish" – and he had his vision of a vast new plan for national development, of roads to resources, of a greening of the tundra, of a country without unemployment and where justice

72

would be done to those regions that had benefited least from the great post-war boom, of a country not bound to the United States but cementing, cock-eyed and crazily, its overseas ties by shifting fifteen percent of our trade to England. His evangelical rhetoric swept the nation, and in Québec, Maurice Duplessis, sensing a winner and seeking revenge, ordered the Union Nationale out in force. In the greatest landslide in history, Diefenbaker won 208 seats, the Liberals 49, the CCF but 8, and Social Credit disappeared as Diefenbaker swept Alberta.

There were substantial accomplishments during the first few years. Millions were poured into the depressed Atlantic provinces and the development of northern resources; prairie farmers fattened their bank accounts with federal aid and the proceeds from massive grain sales to China; the aged, the disabled and veterans benefited from the government's largesse. Though described by Saturday Night as a "sonorous, solidified hunk of Diefenbaker vision," his 1960 Bill of Rights reaffirmed his belief in fundamental freedoms safe from the long arm of government. The same principles, applied to South Africa, led Diefenbaker to encourage its withdrawal from the Commonwealth.

But it was not long before the vision became a mirage. The fault was partly Diefenbaker's, for as it turned out, the skilled courtroom lawyer, the revivalist preacher lacked the experience, the talent, the personality, to lead a government. He distrusted his civil service advisors, refused to delegate authority (or when he did, delegated too much), imposed his will on weak ministers and gave way to strong, was at times impetuous and at others vacillating, trusting few and suspecting many, his course stumbling and erratic. As time passed, decisions were postponed, delayed, changed. The Diefenbaker government seemed immobilized. The recession deepened, unemployment remained high, American investment continued, and the government engaged in a public brawl with the head of the Bank of Canada, James Coyne, over economic policy and finally dismissed him. The Canadian dollar fell, and during the 1962 election the so-called Diefendollar had to be pegged at ninety-two-and-a-half cents. There seemed to be a lack of clarity and consistency in defence policy. There was no one in the cabinet to interpret the new nationalism that had swept Jean Lesage and the likes of René Levesque into Québec power in 1960, and Diefenbaker's advocacy of unhyphenated Canadianism was not only obsolete but ridiculous in the eyes of French Canadians.

Diefenbaker faced a disillusioned electorate in 1962. Rural Canada remained staunchly Conservative, except in Québec, where Réal Caouette with his slogan *Il n'y a rien à perdre* had won 26 seats, but the cities rejected Diefenbaker en masse, even in the prairies. The Chief emerged with 116 seats, enough to retain power as head of a minority government. But not only had he lost the confidence of the country, he had also lost the confidence of many in his party and some in his cabinet.

The uncertainty over defence policy finally brought him down. Soon after taking office, Diefenbaker had cancelled the project to build a Canadian jet, the Avro Arrow, and he had tied Canadian defence policy to the American. He completed the negotiations, begun by the Liberals, to establish NORAD, and had agreed to instal Bomarc missiles as part of Canada's contribution to continental defence. By 1962, the Bomarcs were installed, but Diefenbaker hesitated to arm them with nuclear weapons. Moreover, when the Americans found Soviet missile sites on Cuba and President Kennedy ordered the Red Alert, Diefenbaker faltered. Early in 1963, the exasperated Americans issued a press release correcting or clarifying Diefenbaker's statements regarding nuclear weapons, and within days his Minister of Defence, a supporter of nuclear weapons, resigned. Defeated in the House, his government a mess as other cabinet ministers resigned, even the Tory press turned against him. Diefenbaker again faced the people asking the voters to support him – the beleaguered warrior – against THEM – the Liberals, the traitors, the Americans, and the agents of big business who had helped bring about his downfall. It was a measure of his personal appeal in rural Canada that the Conservatives won 95 seats and the support of one voter in three. But the Liberals won 129 seats and Lester Pearson took office as the head of a minority government.

Diefenbaker remained the Tory chieftain and leader of the

opposition for four years, once again in 1965 preventing the Liberals from winning a majority, and the inept Liberal government provided ample opportunity for him to display his gift for invective and ridicule, but even within the party caucus there was growing dissatisfaction with his leadership. The end came in 1967 when dissident Conservatives forced a leadership convention. Refusing to bow out gracefully, Diefenbaker suffered a final humiliation when he stood fifth on the first ballot. Grim faced, he stayed for another and another, until he finally announced his withdrawal and strode, a broken and tragic figure, from Maple Leaf Gardens.

But the voters of Prince Albert remained loyal, and sent him back to Ottawa to heap scorn and wag his finger at Pearson and Trudeau until his death in Ottawa on August 16, 1979.

The Painting:

I have a vivid impression associated with John Diefenbaker. It is the cancellation of the Avro Arrow. As a young man, I worked at Avro and my father was one of thousands who lost their livelihood that day. The impression is personal and powerful. The Canadian aircraft industry was destroyed when the prototypes were broken up. Canada's current pride in the Manipulator Arm for the space shuttle, and arguments that Canada must develop its high technology industries, are bitterly ironic and heighten my impression of the man. In a sense, he defeated me (with a sucker punch) and got to me at an obvious level.

The red arrow is the Avro Arrow, but it is also his tenure, his squandered opportunity. Diefenbaker was a one-man band who veered into highly personalized style. Everything was centred on him, his vision. He rides or falls, therefore, on the depth of his vision. His vision was a huge bubble blown from a prairie populist's pipe. It popped. The word 'Chief,' partially obscured in the painting, is appropriate: he ended up as Chief of his own tribe, with no warriors, wearing his old headdress to any pow-wow that would have him.

76

The painting is large because he was larger than life, he was 'High Art' caricature. He was a fighter all his life; in the criminal courts, in his quest for office, in his capture of the Prime Minister's office, in his government, and in his final attempts to hold on to his party. He never gave up, an embattled charismatic leader, taking on all comers despite the odds. He was a devastating opponent, from either side of the House, but I remember seeing him on television when I was living in New York, and he looked a little mad: viewing him from the other side of the border, he seemed strange in his tightly tailored suit, with that curly hair, and his head bobbing and weaving like a preacher man who's been hit too many times, full of stern indignation. He looked like a Southern country Senator.

With this painting, I was lucky. I got it the first time, it works. There's no other portrait like it in the group: more would have been like sixteen Henny Youngman one-liners. His personality was his power. So, my name is there, fighting back, for me, for my father.

I T WAS A TUMULTUOUS TIME presided over by a man from the manse. It was a time when rancor and recrimination rode herd, when Lester Bowles Pearson – the decisive negotiator sporting a prim bow tie – seemed swamped in details of disarray: de Gaulle's Vivre le Québec libre, the Hal Banks and Gerda Munsinger scandals, medicare, the Bomarc nuclear warhead debate, the Canada Pension Plan, the flag debate, Expo '67, and Walter Gordon's budgets, René Levesque and *maîtres chez nous*, student radicals, influence peddling, armed forces unification, and the first bombs of the F.L.Q. It was not easy in the mid-60s to keep the country on an even keel, but Lester Pearson kept a shaky hand on the tiller for five years, before turning it over to the younger, firmer grip of Pierre Trudeau.

"Mike" Pearson was born on the outskirts of Toronto in 1897. The son of a Methodist minister, it was inevitable that he would go to Victoria College where he applied himself reasonably diligently to sports and studies until he was old enough to join up. After serving with a hospital unit in the eastern Mediterranean, he switched to the Royal Flying Corps where his squadron leader decided "Mike" was more fitting than Lester. After one-and-a-half hours of instruction, he went on his first solo flight and crashed, got hit by a bus during a London blackout – "I got hurt before I got a chance to get killed" – and was invalided home. Back at University, he took a degree in history and then, after playing semi-pro baseball for a season and a disillusioning experience in a meat factory, he went off to Oxford on a Massey Fellowship. Hockey took more time than history, and he played for Britain's Olympic team, winning from an appreciative Swiss sports writer the name, Herr Zigzag. After Oxford, it was back to Toronto as a lecturer in history, where he preferred coaching the hockey team – replacing Conn Smythe – to working on a book about the United Empire Loyalists. He never finished the book. Marriage, two children, and slow promotions, led him to write the External Affairs examination. He stood first in the exams and in 1928 went to Ottawa as a novice diplomat. Perhaps not the most gifted in the

Department, he nonetheless rose rapidly, and over the next two decades served in London, Geneva, and Washington, before finally reaching diplomat heaven – appointment as Undersecretary of State in 1946.

As a diplomat, Pearson was hard-working during and after hours. He was charming, anxious to please, clear-headed, a good writer and a good speaker, despite a lisp he would never lose. He made friends easily, and cultivated them deliberately. Despite his unassuming manner, he was decidedly ambitious and had a very tough streak. He had a robust sense of humour, including the capacity to laugh at himself. "The King had the honour of meeting me this afternoon at Buckingham Palace," he wrote during a trip to London soon after his appointment.

Pearson was a Canadian nationalist, and during the middle thirties, at least, could be described as an isolationist whose view of Britain and Europe was not unlike Mackenzie King's. But as war approached, after the failure at Munich, he wrote his Ottawa superiors: "My emotional reaction to the events of the last two months is to become an out-and-out isolationist, and yet when I begin to reason it out it isn't as simple as that. In short, I just can't find the answer to a lot of questions…. But if I am tempted to become completely cynical and isolationist, I think of Hitler screeching into the microphone, Jewish women and children in ditches on the Polish border … and then, whatever the British side may represent, the other does indeed stand for savagery and barbarism." Pearson came out of the War against savagery and barbarism as a firm believer in collective security and Canada's important role as a middle power.

When St. Laurent formed his government in September 1948, he asked Pearson, his undersecretary when he was Minister of External Affairs, to accept a safe seat in Algoma and join the cabinet. Asked by reporters when he had become a Liberal, he replied: "Today." Under Pearson, there was none of the hesitation of the Mackenzie King years. Canada pursued a vigorous and positive role at the United Nations, in the formation of NATO, in the Commonwealth, and finally, during the Suez crisis when Pearson's skilful diplomacy won him – and the country – a Nobel Prize. Much to the dismay, even the disgust, of some of his more "political" colleagues who had worked for the party in the trenches, Pearson was the odds-on favourite to succeed St. Laurent when he resigned in 1957.

Pearson had promised "Sixty days of decision" during the '63 election, underlining the indecision of the Diefenbaker government, but on the sixtieth day, Walter Gordon submitted his resignation as Finance Minister. Little that was decisive had been done. There was something shabby and bumbling in the air. Gordon's budget measures, designed to place some controls on foreign investment, were denounced as unwise and unworkable and it was revealed that he had used Bay Street advisors to work on the budget. Gordon survived, but much of the budget was withdrawn. Pearson never did provide the leadership people expected. He presented a picture of nice guy ineptitude, a man who couldn't find the red phone when it rang. His government was scarred by a number of scandals involving his Québec ministers, everything from petty furniture deals to involvement with Mafia dope peddlers. But despite the appearance of stumbling acrimony, the achievements of his five years in office were substantial.

His major concern was Québec, where the election of Jean Lesage and the Liberals in 1960 had ushered in what has been called, *la revolution tranquille*. Québec would no longer pursue the outdated defensive nationalism of the Duplessis era, but a new and positive nationalism where the state would take charge of moulding and protecting a new society. The slogan, *maîtres chez nous,* not only meant that the government would play a more active role within Québec, it also meant that Québec would demand more power and more revenue from Ottawa. Pearson made a number of conciliatory moves: modifications to the Canada Pension Plan to allow Québec to have its own plan, attempts to find an amending formula for the constitution, changes in the federal-provincial tax agreements to give Québec more freedom, and finally the appointment of the famous B and B Commission to examine the state of bilingualism and biculturalism in Canada. Its preliminary report underlined the glaring social and economic inequalities between French and

English, urged the government to adopt the principle of linguistic equality, and warned that French Canadians were increasingly identifying their future with Québec alone. The government moved at once to implement the principle of bilingualism in the federal civil service.

But there seemed no end to Québec's demands. Québec leaders spoke of two nations, equality or independence, associate states, and an increasing number, of complete independence. It was to combat this extreme Québec nationalism and arrest the move towards some form of de facto separation that three outstanding Québécois came to Ottawa in 1965 to help the beleaguered Pearson government: Jean Marchand, the senior of the three, Gérard Pelletier, and Pierre Elliott Trudeau. And it was to lend his support to the nationalist movement that General Charles de Gaulle came to Montreal to deliver his famous Vivre le Quebec libre in 1967. De Gaulle's conduct was unacceptable, declared an outraged Pearson, and the General went home.

The Canada Pension Plan, providing for the first time a universal and contributory old age pension plan backed by a guaranteed income supplement for the needy, was an important addition to our social security system, as were the Canada Assistance Plan to finance child care, mothers allowances, and other income support programs for the poor. Far more controversial was the introduction of medicare, which the Pearson government more or less forced on the provinces and shoved down the throat of an unhappy medical profession.

One of Pearson's proudest moments was when the Canadian flag, "his" Canadian flag (though at first he wanted three red maple leafs and two blue exterior bars), was raised on Parliament Hill. It had only been approved after a long and incredibly nasty debate, as John Diefenbaker scorched the rafters with his denunciation of those who would sell short the Union Jack and the British connection. But it was fitting that the Canadian flag flew over Expo 67 when Canada celebrated its hundredth birthday and was proudly and lavishly host to the world. But Mike Pearson, the nationalist, was wary of adopting too nationalistic a stance against the United States (his relations with U.S. Presidents went from Kennedy's patronizing, "He'll do," to Johnson's scathing anger after Pearson opposed American bombing in North Vietnam). The ties of trade with the U.S. were so strong, the need for investment capital so great, that he kept a lid on Walter Gordon's nationalist enthusiasms. Indeed, if anything, the Pearson government moved closer towards integration when it negotiated the automobile pact in 1965, which secured for Canada a much greater share of automobile production while creating an integrated continental automobile industry.

But the electorate was never that impressed with Mike Pearson's government. Whatever its accomplishments, its appearance was sloppy and rumpled. In 1965, when Pearson asked the voters to return a majority government, they sent back a parliament virtually unchanged. After presiding over the nation's centennial, Pearson announced his retirement. On April 19, 1968, two weeks after Pierre Trudeau had won the Liberal leadership, he resigned as Prime Minister. He died in Ottawa on December 27, 1972.

The Painting:

Pearson was difficult, a challenge. I couldn't pin him down in my mind. I tried this painting three times. He was a bright and accomplished man, but he was never accused of flamboyance. His powers were hidden to the casual observer. When I was in New York, the place was packed every time Pearson spoke at the United Nations General Assembly. He was, at that time, the only Canadian politician I can remember reading about in the New York Times.

I thought of basing the painting on the flag, for which he will certainly be remembered, but that was too simple. He was a complex man, thought of as amiable and affable, a 'nice guy,' but he was no weakling. He could be hard-nosed when he had to be.

The first version was too meditative, all washes, a diptych. The next was bombastic, black, white and red, a fragmented flag. The painting I ended up with is totally different in feeling, yellow ochre

Working study: oil 15" × 12"

and brown from the lighter end of the colour scale. This horizon has little soft explosions in it. The twin streams of blue and green are like the currents which directed the flow of Pearson's life: academia and diplomacy. The diagonal strokes in a left-handed direction are the sinister, tough threads of his character. They are not bombastic or vivid, and seemed to me the colour essence of Pearson. The flag could not be ignored. When you see it flying away from home, it matters. There is a blue flag which I put in at the end. This painting could not be flat. Pearson was too full of energy and intelligence, his political life too tumultuous, but as a whole, the painting has gentleness.

J OE CLARK stands like a Tory-blue sliver in the middle of the Trudeau years, a young man who made an incredible leap from nowhere, and then skidded to a halt. "Ideally, what the party is looking for is a leader who can heal the splits between right and left and between central Canada and the west, who can make strides in Québec and who has charisma." That's what a veteran journalist wrote the day before the Conservatives gathered in Ottawa in February, 1976, to select a new leader. After all, Robert Stanfield had been given three chances to rid the land of Pierre Trudeau. Eleven candidates claimed they could lead the Tories out of the doldrums and the desert. On the fourth ballot, they selected Joe Clark, the boy from High River. He was thirty-six.

Clark called himself a journalist in the Parliamentary Guide, but apart from writing columns for the High River Times, published by his father, editing the University of Alberta student newspaper, and working during the summer for the Canadian Press and the Edmonton Journal, he had no journalistic experience. Indeed, he had no experience outside of politics. In a way it was incredible: a young man who'd never really had a job, who'd never managed anything, was supposed to be ready to manage the country. At university, he had been active in the student Conservative Party, which he'd led in the mock Parliament; his adversary – the Liberal Prime Minister – was Jim Coutts, later a Man About Power in the Liberal Prime Minister's office. As it turned out, the mysteries of law at both Dalhousie and British Columbia were too great or too boring for a young man obsessed with politics, and although he ultimately got an MA in Political Science, he spent the sixties as president of the Conservative student federation, working for Davie Fulton in B.C. and Peter Lougheed in Alberta, failing to win his seat in the 1967 Alberta provincial election, and finally working for three years as an aide to Robert Stanfield. In 1972, he ran successfully in his home riding of Rocky Mountain, and became a hard-working Tory backbencher.

The favourites at the 1976 convention were Claude Wagner and Brian Mulroney, and in a field of eleven, Clark ranked near the bottom. But while some candidates pursued the media, Clark pursued the delegates, seeking support when their favourite had been knocked out. The strategy worked. A distant third on the first ballot, Clark picked up support from those who wanted neither of the favourites and won on the fourth ballot by 65 votes. There was no great enthusiasm for the new leader, and there were continual rumblings within the party. His image – and that's all he was at that stage, an image on the political make – was one of awkwardness. It was played up by the press. "Joe Who," became a political buzz-word, and there was a spate of Joe Clark jokes. Tripping up stairs or losing his suitcase while abroad didn't help. Though a tall man, he looked small on television. There seemed no way he could lead a divided and disgruntled party to victory over Pierre Trudeau.

But by 1979, the voters had lost confidence in the Liberals, and particularly in Pierre Trudeau, who seemed a pale shadow of his promise. In a surprising verdict, they returned Joe Clark at the head of a minority government. Not surprisingly, he preferred a group approach to decision making, expanding the Committee system in caucus. But his caucus support was uncertain. The government was soon in disarray. He had to back down on his pre-election promise to move the Canadian embassy from Tel Aviv to Jerusalem. He watched helplessly as the inflation rate reached a then historic high of 14 percent. His promises to "privatize" PetroCan and other crown corporations were easier made than done, and he seemed too willing to sell the national government short in his dealings with the provinces. Although Trudeau had resigned as Liberal leader soon after the election, or perhaps because of it, the polls soon showed an upsurge of Liberal support. When John Crosbie brought down his realistic "Short-term pain for Long-term Gain" budget in November – with its eighteen cent tax on a gallon of gasoline – the Liberals seized the opportunity to try and defeat the government. Clark, who had convinced his ministers that they should govern as if they had a majority, miscalculated Liberal intentions and refused to make necessary

concessions to the five Socred members from Québec. The Tories were defeated.

The Liberals brought Trudeau out of mothballs, sloughing aside the old "gunslinger" image, so he could conduct a low-key campaign, saying so little in speeches so numbing that they were works of craft, promising that this would be his last. Liberals promoted Trudeau as the only man who could keep Québec within confederation, and Ontario voters deserted a government that promised higher energy prices. It was an inglorious campaign, but the Liberals won all but one seat in Québec, and with a decisive victory in Ontario, were returned to power. When he resigned, Joe Clark had been Prime Minister for 272 days.

For three years, Joe Clark tried to retain his position as Conservative leader, performing effectively in the Commons, securing important changes to Trudeau's bill of rights, working hard at what he knew how to do: consolidating the party pros, hacks and flacks. But opposition mounted as Conservatives became increasingly convinced that Clark could never be a winner. Finally, in 1983, he grasped the nettle, demanded a vote of confidence, and when that was not forthcoming to the extent he desired, called a leadership convention. His chief opponent was the handsome, slick-talking, bilingual one-time head of the Iron Ore Company, Brian Mulroney. Many delegates were convinced that, whatever his fine personal qualities, Clark could only lose, and Mulroney won the post he had so long schemed for and coveted. At 44, Joe Clark was back in the Tory trenches. Perhaps he felt, like Arthur Meighen, that the party would turn to him again.

The Painting:

The painting happened in one instant, a little like Clark's career, but it took a year to refine to its final state.

I wanted to avoid taking an easy shot at Clark, the "Joe Who" converted in 1981 to "Joe Why." He was having a hard time in the Party and in the media when I was working on him. A 12' x 1' canvas, all grey, would have been wrong, stupid. Anyone who becomes Prime Minister has to have something special.

Time has changed my opinion of Clark. I was in Ottawa one morning, at breakfast, and we came face to face. Our eyes met and I felt a warmth, wit and intelligence about him that I hadn't seen on television. I had judged him through the media, but face to face I felt something different. He was the youngest, up against the toughest and brightest, one of the top three Prime Ministers. In that company, Clark proved, through hard circumstances, to be a stable character, courageous.

The painting is special among the group. It is two panels, eight feet by one foot, mounted on masonite separated by the centre stripe, which is Tory blue, indicating his tenacity, his guts. The two outside panels are pastel colours, colours I imagined in the foothills of the springtime Rockies, bursting with life and new growth. The white lines are like calligraphy and provide a sense of probing for the establishment of new directions, but they don't connect because of the separation of the blue. The blue is the Tories themselves, splitting wide open, as they frequently do.

87

CANADIANS RAVED about Pierre Trudeau or reviled him. The nation was awash with Trudeaumania or Trudeauphobia. No other leader aroused such intensity. He became a pervasive, some said perverse, presence. He persuaded, bullied, prodded, romanced, sneered at and swore at Canadians, treating them with affection or contempt, confronting them with his view of the nation, challenging them to an intellectual debate or a political brawl. He did not allow apathy.

For a man so public, he remained an enigma, cross-cut by contradictions: playful and stern, sophisticated and vulgar, witty and flat-footed, charming and abusive, vaguely amiable but always remote, a press man's delight but contemptuous of the press, an intellectual often surrounded by political hacks, a zealous reformer who rewarded his friends and punished his enemies with little apparent regard for the public good, a man of endless paradoxes, of so many pieces that he left the people – even when they applauded – mystified.

His biographer, George Radwanski, would like us to believe that Trudeau, the cold rationalist, lacking in sensitivity or empathy for the feelings of others, is all front. "At his core," he says, "Pierre Trudeau is not a passionless man, but one with so much emotion that he has rigorously walled it in; not arrogant and thick-skinned, but rather so vulnerable that he has erected a barrier of remoteness that only a trusted few can penetrate; not inflated with confidence and with a sense of his own power, but quite unassuming and even, in certain situations, curiously unsure of himself." The explanation, it seems, lies in his boyhood. Physically frail, he forced himself to become a superbly conditioned athlete, which he still is. Afraid he might be intellectually inferior, he worked harder, and developed a fierce competitiveness that moved from fear of being left behind to a determination to be at the front. So sensitive that he burst easily into tears, he built up the defensive walls that so few have penetrated. Trudeau grew up competitive, inner-directed, with enormous powers of self-discipline. He was also intellectually alive, enormously curious, determined to experience the fullest range of physical, intellectual, and aesthetic experiences – parachute skiing, Shanghai as it fell to Mao Tse Tung, Tibetan meditations, love and life with a flower child, and the Prime Ministership of Canada.

As a young man, too, he developed that fierce sense of independence, that desire for freedom, that at its worst became an immature rebelliousness and at its best an intense commitment to individual freedom and a course of political action. As a youth, he rebelled against his teachers, current fashions, any form of established authority in the church or state. As a man, he could state that, "I have never been able to accept any discipline except that which I imposed upon myself – and there was a time when I used to impose it often. For, in the art of living, as in that of loving, or of governing – it is all the same – I found it unacceptable that others should claim to know better than I what was good for me." Distrusting ideology, he declared in 1967 that the "only constant factor to be found in my thinking over the years has been opposition to accepted opinions.... My political action, or my theory – insomuch as I can be said to have one – can be expressed very simply: create counterweights."

He was born Joseph Phillippe Pierre Ives Elliott Trudeau in Montréal on October 18, 1919, the eldest son of Grace Elliott and Charles Trudeau. His mother, though half-French and fluently bilingual, was essentially English. His father, a wealthy businessman, fun-loving and gregarious, a poker-playing Conservative, loved sports and owned a large chunk of the Montréal Royals baseball team. He died when Pierre Elliott was fifteen, a loss, writes Radwanski, that hurt the son "so deeply that he still cannot talk about it without visible emotion." He grew up in a bilingual and bicultural environment, though more French than English and fervently Roman Catholic. After eight years at the Jesuit College Jean de Brébeuf, he studied law at Montréal and after being called to the bar in 1943, pursued post-graduate studies in economics, political science and law at Harvard, Paris and the London School of Economics. Before returning to Canada in 1949, he set out on an eighteen month trek around the world: arrested in Palestine, crossing a Burma torn by civil war, riding with French troops in Indo-China, and watching the Communists take Shanghai.

Back in Canada, he worked for St. Laurent for three years in Ottawa, but became increasingly involved in the struggle for democracy in Québec. In 1949, he marched with the workers in the famous Asbestos strike, and was ordered out of town by Duplessis' police. The next year, he and Gérard Pelletier and others founded Cité Libre, a magazine devoted to the modernization and democratization of Québec, defying the power of both church and state. Trudeau and Cité Libre were among the forces of reform that brought Jean Lesage and the Liberals to power in 1960, but it was not long before he became apprehensive and then sharply critical of the form and direction the new nationalism was taking in Québec, writing contemptuously of the "New Treason of the Intellectuals" and of "The Separatist Counter-Revolutionaries," denouncing the nostrums of special status, two nations, and independence. By 1965, despite his earlier condemnation of Pearson for taking nuclear arms, he joined his old friends Jean Marchand and Gérard Pelletier as Liberal MPs in Ottawa to combat the menace of Québec nationalism. A reformed federal system and a national government that reflected the linguistic and cultural partnership between French and English would be the counterweight to the forces of Québec nationalism threatening the future of the country, and, in his mind, the tyranny of a state based on the ideologies of ethnicity or race.

Soon after his arrival in Ottawa, Trudeau became parliamentary secretary to the Prime Minister, and a year later Minister of Justice. Not everyone supported his efforts to liberalize the law on divorce, abortion and homosexuality, but his comment that "the state has no business in the bedrooms of the nation" certainly captured the mood of the post-war generation. But his major responsibility was handling the sensitive question of constitutional reform where, in English-Canadian eyes, he emerged as the French Canadian who was prepared to stand up to Québec. "No more of this open-ended negotiation.... This is the idea of Munich. It may be we need a showdown." His was a fresh new image, a new outspokenness, a manner and language that suited the times. A dark horse candidate at the beginning of the leadership campaign in 1968, he had the advantage of being the only French Canadian in the race. There were many who believed that Trudeau lacked the experience, the stability, the breadth necessary to lead the party and the country, but they were narrowly outnumbered by those who believed he offered the promise of a new beginning, a candid and open approach to politics, symbolized by the turtle-neck and sandals not the three-piece pin-stripe suit. On April 6, Pierre Trudeau became the seventh leader of the Liberal party since Confederation, and on April 20 the sixth Liberal Prime Minister. The fifteen year love-hate relationship with Canadians had begun.

Canada and Trudeau have come a long way since 1968: through the crisis provoked by the FLQ, the election of René Levesque and the separatist referendum; through the implementation of bilingualism in federal institutions, the outrage (on both sides) over the air traffic controllers strike, his inability to curry any kind of favour in the West, and the Charter of Rights and Freedoms – attempting within limits to entrench our legal rights and civil liberties in the fundamental law of the land, guaranteeing the linguistic equality of all Canadians; through the break-up of his marriage, the Nixon shock, the oil shocks, the internal conflict over energy policy, and the toughest economic times since the '30s; through a reassessment of our foreign policy, the recognition of China, the crises in southeast Asia and Afghanistan, the debate over nuclear weapons, and the globe-trotting initiative to find a way, if not to peace, at least away from a nuclear war – or as the cynics would say, to go out on a high roll.

Canadians were curiously ambivalent about Pierre Trudeau. The West became increasingly hostile, and by 1980 Liberal Canada ended at Winnipeg and the rest seemed irrevocably lost as long as he remained in power. Ontario was far more fickle, revising its position each time he faced the country between 1968 and 1980, and by 1984 seemed about to reverse itself again. Only Québec remained consistently faithful, despite the fulminations of the péquistes.

Few knew what to make of Pierre Trudeau. Perhaps it was too much to believe that one man wearing a rose in his lapel could bring

French and English together, redress regional inequalities, enrich the poor without impoverishing the rich – whether individuals or provinces – crush the terrorists of the FLQ without tramping on civil liberties, bring a logic and a rationality to government without destroying its humanity, lead a political party without yielding to the imperatives of politicians, and submitting to a torrent of abuse without responding in kind. What were people to make of a man who, instead of sneaking down secret back stairwells, slid down staircases, drove a Mercedes 300 SL, paddled an arctic canoe, pirouetted behind the Queen, gave Canadians the finger, told striking taxi drivers "mange la merde," called opposition MPS "nobodies," bridled at authority and imposed it with impunity, mouthed an epithet across the floor of the Commons bowdlerized for Hansard as "fuddle duddle," fathered two sons on Christmas Day, and endured the public spectacle of his estranged wife with incredible patience and dignity.

Whatever the ultimate verdict of history, there was no doubt that he had forced us to look into the depths of our psyche as Canadians, testing our courage as well as our patience, uniting us at times but dividing us at others. But whatever the divided nation thought of him, they knew he was no local boy doing figure-eights on a small pond. He was a man of the larger world. He seemed never locked into his past or the nation's, and perhaps only a man so independent of mind and so fascinated by the future could so often, and so maddeningly, shrug at the present.

The Painting:

Pierre Trudeau is a shy man but a natural performer, a man with incredible personal style, engaging and abrasive, subdued and ebullient, accessible and cold and remote, and warm.

I tried painting Trudeau three times. The first was almost all white, with canvases stacked on top of each other. For some reason, I tried "stacking" Laurier as well, but that Trudeau was too papal. The

second attempt was his early years, the flashy glory days. Well, glory days are glory days, gone, and so is that version of a man I admire. Internationally, he has given us a stature we've never had.

I decided on the ten'-by-six' proportion to underscore Trudeau's presence, ten feet high. The image is marginally related to my 1958 painting, "The Visitor." It also had an enigmatic quality, a slightly threatening air. The Maltese Cross is obviously a form I like. It is used here because of Trudeau's religion. His Jesuit education had a strong bearing on his life. The intellectual discipline from Jean de Brébeuf College is in his bones, but the halo-like cross is slipping a bit.

The painting has two sections; the division runs from upper right to bottom left. The right side is softer. Trudeau has a gentle side to him, seen when he is with his children. Trudeau is not finished yet,

he will go on to play some part, perhaps internationally. I could still add one or two panels, panels in the mind, the future.

The other side is hard, rigid, disciplined, but not entirely so. Trudeau has too much heart to be totally hard-edged. He can be explosive. His life seems dominated by logic, but emotion bursts through. I have often used borders in my paintings, but here, for the first time, there's only half a border. It contains a blue reminiscent of the Québec flag and gives that side of the painting, as an integral part of the whole, a more structured and firmer sense. The division is, in part, a device to make the painting work.

The stripes are entirely hard-edged and bold, like Trudeau's discipline, strength and authority. A huge head-shape floats above the field of stripes. Everything about Trudeau seems centered on his mind. The head dominates. The things that look like cogs are actually part of a construction drawing of the female form. The head-shape has its back turned to a three-quarters profile. It is commanding, remote and removed. The black and grey – severe, powerful and even ominous colours – emphasize dominance and distance, while remaining enigmatic. The awkwardness is deliberate. I did not try to pretty it up. Trudeau has incredible eyes, brilliant and sharp, like a fox's. He seems able to look through you. The eyes in the painting are like him, always seeing. The second set are akin to the mind's eye, the eye that imagines what is beyond the seen.